The Miraculous Adventures of Willy Maze

a novel

Howard J. Zeger

Sunbridge Books
Deerfield Beach, Florida

This is a work of fiction. All names, characters, places, and incidents were fabricated from the author's imagination, or used fictitiously.

For Kathy

Chapter 1

Before my spirit body departed the celestial realm, I consulted with the benevolent prophet of great wisdom, truth, love and compassion. After he gave me instructions for my new assignment, I bravely traveled the 500 billion miles to the oceanic blue-green planet that orbited the sun. With atomic-like speed, I entered earth's atmosphere through black-gray clouds, glided over Antarctica, bypassed the Andes, climbed the Himalayas, crossed the stormy Atlantic, swam New York's Hudson River north to south, and then finally entered a hospital room, where a young mother, Etta Maze, just gave birth to a healthy baby boy: me, William Edgar Maze. My father, Harry, proudly stood nearby while a brilliant blue light filled the room a few moments. The obstetrician spanked my bottom; I drew my first breath, and the divine spirit of God entered my tiny pink lungs.

That took place in 1956, three o'clock, on a Tuesday afternoon in an unusually cold September. Silvery white snowflakes softly dropped as my mother and father lovingly wrapped me in a wool shawl before leaving Saint Lukes Hospital, in Newburgh, N.Y. They carried me across Dubois Street, and into our warm home nearby. And on that day, the miraculous adventures of little Willy Maze had begun.

Eight days passed, when a man came to visit. He had a long black beard, a round fur hat, wool overcoat, scarf, and carried a scratched leather satchel. He spoke with my mother and father while I happily sucked my thumb in a crib, paying little attention, until my mother removed my clean diaper, put me on a towel-covered pillow, and then my father supported it from underneath. My mother poured whiskey onto my rubber pacifier, and she placed it in my mouth. It tasted good and made me feel numb. The man stood over me, holding a sharp and shiny object. I warily watched as he said something in another language, grasped my little wee-wee, and then I felt something extremely painful. I screamed so loud the man's black hat blew off his head and onto the floor. He put it back on, wiped the blood off my wee-wee, and then bandaged it. He left the house while my mother placed the liquor-soaked pacifier into my mouth again. And that was one day in my life, I never wanted to remember.

During the winter of 1957, we celebrated my first birthday. My parents brought me outside in a baby carriage, so I could watch the neighborhood children and adults sleigh ride down the long, snow-covered hill on Dubois Street. The bottom intersected with Broadway and crossed over to William Street, where Harry's, my father's kosher delicatessen was located. The freezing wind reddened my cheeks and made my nose feel as cold as an icicle. That's when I first realized I had these strange powers: the ability to shut off sound, and to leave my body and travel anywhere I wanted. It's called an out-of-body-experience, or astral travel. All I had to do was close my eyes, think of the place I wanted to be, and then go there in my astral, or spirit body.

The second year of my life came and went so fast, I don't even recall what took place.

On my third birthday while my mother aimed a movie camera, I made a wish and blew out the candles on a chocolate cake. The three of us ate a slice with a scoop of vanilla ice cream. Afterward, mom dressed me in warm clothes and insulated boots, and dad took me sleigh riding down Dubois Street. On our first run, he lost control of the sled and we crashed into a snowbank plowed against the curb. The white, powdery freeze found its way inside my coat collar and down my neck. God, that was a shocking experience! We laughed, brushed ourselves off, and then rode the steep hill to the bottom.

On a blizzardy winter day while I was playing in the living room, a program about Florida came on the television. I watched children swim in the ocean, make sandcastles, and collect colorful seashells along a golden beach. There was no snow in sight. They said on the television, the place was called Miami Beach. I wanted to go there, so I went upstairs to my room, rested my head on a pillow, closed my eyes, and then thought about the place. The next thing I knew, I was out of my body and riding on a train. I had sunshades on, carried a small suitcase packed with a beach towel and a bathing suit; a baseball cap on my head, flipflops on my feet, and a train ticket in my hand. I was on my way south. I entered the bar-car and asked the bartender for a soda, when I noticed a familiar-looking gentleman seated at the bar with two beautiful young ladies on either side of him. He smoked a cigar and glanced down at me. I recognized his face from watching television. It was Larry, from *The Three Stooges*.

I looked up at him and asked, "Can I get your autograph mister?"

The man smiled at one of the women beside him, borrowed a pen from the bartender, and then scrawled his name on a cocktail napkin. He reached down and put it in my little hand.

"Here you go young man."

"Thank you."

"You're welcome. Do you know who I am?" he asked, gazing at me with his black eyes and drinking something from a glass with ice cubes in it.

I looked at his wild, reddish-brown hair and replied: "You're Larry, from *The Three Stooges*. I watch your show almost every day."

"That's right. And what's your name?"

"Willy Maze."

"It was nice meeting you, Willy. Now go back to your mother and father. They're probably wondering where you went."

Glowing inside, I left the bar car, happily took the napkin back to my seat, and then proudly admired the autograph.

Larry Fine

An older boy curtly asked from the seat next to me. "What's that?"

"An autograph from one of *The Three Stooges*," I answered while excitedly showing it to him.

The older kid became jealous, grabbed one end of the napkin and pulled it away from me; it was torn in half and the signature was ruined. The boy smirked while I cried. I dropped the ripped napkin as the boy's mother and father apathetically stood by and watched.

I closed my eyes, found myself in my bedroom again, and then dismally looked out the window at the snow and ice-covered trees in the front yard.

By the age of four, I made my first visit to Downing Park in the city of Newburgh. I loved the summer days at the pond, the concert band, the graceful swans, the royal feathered peacocks, and the talkative Canadian ducks and ducklings. A man fed pigeons by the water while thick clumps of dandelion and red clover blossoms blanketed the grass in the park. The birds, bees, and butterflies fluttered all around me.

On my second visit to the park, my mother showed me the colossal boulders there. I would climb them, and my mom would take photographs of me on top.

Afterward, we hiked up a hill where I played by an old Indian fort. That's where I first heard the strange voice on the wind. It called through branches of a tall oak tree. Perhaps in a language an Indian would speak.

"Who's that, Mom?"

"I don't know, William. Come on. Let's go down to Broadway. I'll buy you a hamburger and a cold soda at Woolworths."

Before we left the fort that day, I heard the talking through the trees once more. In English. "We'll meet again, young Willy."

That coming winter my parents took me to the frozen pond in Downing Park, where they taught me how to skate. While the chilly evening approached, I observed the colorful Christmas lights on the houses and trees on Third Street. I listened while bells jingled, signaling the times were joyful yet fleeting.

When Spring arrived, my father and I watched the marching bands parade down Broadway. I got chills up and down my spine as men and women blasted sounds through their trumpets, trombones, sousaphones, French horns, and tubas. The percussionists bashed their drums and crashed their cymbals, making my backbone tingle with electricity. I knew then I wanted to learn more about this thing called music. At home I started drumming on pots, pans, boxes, and buckets. Driving my parents crazy.

Chapter 2

On November 8, 1960, John Fitzgerald Kennedy had been elected the 35th president of the United States. I was barely old enough to know what a president was.

By the age of six, I entered kindergarten at Broadway School in Newburgh, and a few months later, our family moved to the suburbs in New Windsor, five miles away. I couldn't understand why we left Newburgh; I loved it there. In the beginning I heartily voiced my discontent about the move, but what could a six-year-old do? I tried running away from home with a baseball glove, hat, and a paper bag filled with snacks, but that didn't get me far, only across the street to an empty lot with dark woods and a train trestle nearby. Under a clear night sky, I crouched behind a small boulder and cried for an hour, until the next-door neighbor found me and walked me home. I got over it.

We lived in a brick, split-level house on Oak Street, across from other homes that had train tracks bordering their backyards. The neighborhood kids and I once played in the acres of thick woods on the other side of the tracks. Memories of laughter bounded through a farmer's corn field past our dead-end street.

Up the road and down Union Avenue, was a town hall, playground with a tennis court, punch ball and basketball courts. A baseball field and dugouts right nearby. Over a chain link fence, rows of apple trees grew all the way up to Windsor Highway.

In 1963, I first learned how to play a musical instrument. It wasn't the drums like I was so enthusiastic about; my parents saw to that. An older cousin of mine didn't want his clarinet, so I ended up with it. The very first time I blew into the instrument, the most heavenly sound came out. I was hooked. I started music lessons, and joined the school band.

On November 22nd of that year, I'll never forget coming home from New Windsor School; the bus driver had the radio on, when she suddenly stopped the yellow vehicle along a street not far from where I lived. She got up off her seat, turned around, and with a stone-cold look on her face announced: *"President Kennedy was assassinated twenty minutes ago."*

After hearing the tragic news, I felt as if a great light had been turned off. I'm not sure if it was ever turned on again.

In 1968, Elvis Presley moved his hips and sang on the TV, while the Reverend Martin Luther King spoke to a crowd in Memphis Tennessee. Some crazy shot him, and his life abruptly ended. Another great and important light for humanity extinguished. On the radio, Bobby Zimmerman sang in a Woody Guthrie-like voice: *and the times they are a changing.'*

The Viet Nam War was raging, and thousands of young men and a small number of women returned home in body bags.

By the age of 13, I saved enough money from working at my father's deli, and I purchased my second Beatles album and a brand-new phonograph from K-Mart; the record cover was all white. I continued taking music lessons on the clarinet, jamming to rock n roll on the record player.

Summer vacation came, and I was in the kitchen, listening to the news on the radio. There was going to be a music festival in the Catskills. *Woodstock '69* they called it.

"I wanna go, Mom."

"Where?"

"To Woodstock. They're having a big music festival up there soon."

"That's too far away, Willy. It's two hours to the Catskills—how would you get there?"

"By car. We could all go. Maybe take a vacation."

"Your father has to work at the deli—we have bills to pay. And don't you have a big baseball game tomorrow?"

"Yeah."

"Your teammates still teasing you about that famous black baseball player, Willie Mays?"

"Yeah, Mom. Everyone teases me. Even the coaches. I keep reminding them my name's spelled different, but they ignore me. I wouldn't be missed. It's not like I'm the team's most valuable player. I strike out almost every time I'm at bat. I could take a bus to Woodstock."

"I don't know why you have such a hard time hitting the ball, Willy. Maybe you should get glasses."

"Mom. Please. I'm not gonna wear glasses playing baseball."

"Your father won't let you ride a bus by yourself to Monticello. You'll watch it on the television."

"It won't be televised, Mom. And it's not just a concert. It's supposed to be a once-in-life time event. I don't see why I can't go."

I observed my mother stand by the sink, and pensively look out the kitchen window.

"I'll ask your father when he comes home. Why don't you practice your clarinet."

"I did this morning for two hours while you went shopping."

"The lawn needs cutting."

"I'll do it tomorrow. I could ride my bike to the music festival."

"Don't be ridiculous. Eat your lunch, William."

After mowing the lawn, I played tackle football in a big field by my house: Eddie, Louie, Joe, and Doug on one team; Frank, Wayne, Anthony, and I, played on the other. After our team kicked ass, Wayne and I rode our bikes around New Windsor a few miles.

I came home, drank ice-cold lemonade while my mother prepared supper. She finished, and went to the living room and noticed through the picture window that the mailman had driven past. She took a cigarette and a lighter and walked down the driveway and retrieved some envelopes and the *Evening News*. Her daily routine in the late afternoon.

Meanwhile, at Harry's Deli, my father opened the cash register, counted his day's earnings, and then placed it in a leather pouch. He grabbed a bag with cold cuts and potato salad, and threw a light switch on the wall before locking the door. He sat in his powder blue Chevrolet, drove along a cobblestoned William Street, and then crossed the bridge into New Windsor, passing a crowded Gus's Tavern while singing a melody from the *Fiddler on the Roof* musical: *"If I were a rich man . . ."*

At the supper table that evening, I impatiently picked at my food, nibbling on some while my father glanced over at me.

"Why aren't you eating, Willy?"

"I'm not crazy about stuffed cabbage, Dad."

"It's good for you. Eating it might improve your batting average," he sarcastically said.

"Dad, please."

"He wants to go to the Catskills, Harry."

"What's in the Catskills, Etta?"

"Woodstock."

"Never mind the Catskills, Willy. You need to clean out the garage. Did you practice your clarinet today?"

"Yeah. Why can't I go, Dad?"

"Because I said so. Finish your supper—you got a baseball game tomorrow."

"Yeah, I know."

While I washed the dishes my parents sat in the living room and watched Dan Rather speak about the hippy music festival on the evening news. It officially kicked off that evening, and about 300,000 people were already there, camped out on Max Yasgur's sprawling dairy farm. And many more were on the way. The news report also showed people stuck on a traffic-clogged New York State Thruway, trying to get to the event.

My mother called from the living room: "It's on, Willy!"

"What?" I asked while watching the water drain from the kitchen sink.

"Woodstock."

I quickly dried my hands, hurried to the living room, and then sat on a chair close to the television set. Under a still shining sun at half past six, a massive audience of young women and men with long hair and tie-dyed tee shirts were dancing and swaying to music performed by a young black man named Richie Havens. He was strumming on a Gibson guitar and singing his heart out.

The television cameras then focused on a half a million in the audience.

"I really wanna go, Mom."

"I told you before, Willy. You're too young. You'll go in a few years."

"They won't have it then."

"Where do you wanna go, Willy?" My father asked as he saw some women near the stage remove their tops and bras, flaunting their various sized breasts. He viewed them with a secret interest.

"The music festival, Dad. The one on the news right now."

"Are you nuts? Those are crazy long-haired hippies—turn the channel, Willy—*Jeopardy* is on."

"Don't you wanna see the naked women, Harry?" Mom teasingly asked.

I changed the channel to the game show and heard a contestant wager on *Jeopardy* before climbing the stairs to my bedroom.

"Psychedelics for $200, please, Alex."

Resting on my bed, I drearily stared at a spot on the bedroom ceiling. I couldn't stop thinking about Woodstock. *Even if I couldn't physically go, I could still astral travel there. I'd only be gone for a few hours and be back home in bed before mom and dad woke up in the morning.* I studied a map of New York State, and found the town of Bethel, the place in the Catskills where the music festival was held. I darkened the lamp in the bedroom, visualized the music festival I had seen on the television earlier, and then felt my astral body leave my physical body. I hovered above the bed, briefly glanced down at my mortal self, and then passed through my open bedroom window.

A fat yellow moon hung in front of me while I journeyed north by northwest on the roadless astral plane. By the speed of thought, I traveled over Route 17, and in a moment or two, reached the bucolic Catskill Mountains of Sullivan County.

Far below me on the roadside: a few thousand parked cars, trucks, vans, buses, and a myriad of people traversed the country lane toward the concert grounds.

I landed on a soft cow pasture, where a purple neon sign welcomed me to Woodstock '69. I mingled between thousands while loud music blared from tall stacks of speakers on both ends of a stage. I found myself in an area filled with other astral travelers, wandering seers, yogis standing on their heads, bodhisattvas, mystics, priests, Chasidim, and ascended masters, (souls who had evolved into higher spiritual beings).

In the air above me, I saw a beautiful being with female features and iridescent blue butterfly wings. She had illuminated colored wheels on the front of her ethereal body. A garland of flowers crowned her head. She landed beside me.

"Hi, Willy. I'm Chakra. Welcome to Woodstock."

"How do you know me?"

"We met in heaven once—I'm your guardian spirit."

"Is that like an angel?"

"We have our similarities. Would you like to dance?"

"I'm not a very good dancer to tell you the truth."

"That's okay—I can teach you," Chakra said. "Why don't we levitate over to the stage—we'll have a much better view of the band from there."

The exciting rock and roll music filled the cool mountain air while my guardian spirit and I danced till the early morning hours.

Prior to leaving the music festival, she introduced me to someone of great authority and importance. He was like no man I had ever seen. His eyes glowed like stars. His white hair and beard hung to the ground. He wore a long silver gown, and a multi-colored skullcap. His feet shone like lightning.

"This is the prophet of love, wisdom, truth and compassion," my guardian spirit said. "And this is the young man they call Willy Maze, your holiness."

"Yes, I know. Greetings, Mr. Maze. I'm pleased you are following your assignment. Your guardian spirit will guide and help you through this life, but you alone must take responsibility for your thoughts and actions. Be sure to obey the Lord's commandments, and the Law of Karma: *Every action—has a reaction*. I have much more to say, but not at this time. I will visit you again when you are older. Till then, farewell. And may God keep you."

I observed the prophet as he stepped onto a white cloud and vanished into the golden rays of sunup.

The early morning dew glistened like jade while a young Jerry Garcia and the Grateful Dead band performed. Their twangy electric guitars, vocals, piano, drums and bass thundered through Yasgur's farmland while my guardian spirit and I had our last dance.

I rose in the air, observed a million souls below, and then visualized my bedroom back home. I passed through the picture window in the living room, got back in bed, and my etheric body manifested into my physical body.

I smelled freshly brewed coffee downstairs while my mother made French toast. A Beatle song played on the radio, *'While My Guitar Gently Weeps.'* I showered, dressed, and then went downstairs and joined my parents for breakfast. My father had his nose buried in a newspaper.

"Morning, William. You sleep well?" my mother inquired.

"Like a baby. Good morning."

"French toast?"

"Sure. I went to Woodstock last night, Mom. It was amazing."

"Was it a nice dream?"

"It wasn't a dream. I was really there."

My father looked up at me while he closed the morning paper. "What did you say, Willy?"

"I was at Woodstock, Dad. The music festival."

"Crazy, long-haired hippies! Pour me another coffee, Etta."

Chapter 3

After working a few hours at the deli, I unlocked my ten-speed and raced down Broadway. I rolled through an abandoned Water Street, taking the scenic route along the Hudson River; it was a gorgeous sunny afternoon, not a cloud above. I suddenly recalled how my guardian spirit's colorful wheels spun, and my astral travel to the music festival the night before. *What a trip.* I changed gears, sweated up Route 9W, onto Union Avenue, passed the cemetery, crossed the railroad tracks by the town hall, and then cruised home on Oak Street.

After a shower, I stood in front of the bedroom mirror with my uniform on. I loved playing baseball. If I could only hit the damn thing, aside for fouls. I had one single in fifteen games. It was the last game of the senior league season. My team, the Yanks, were tied with the Cornwall Tigers for first place. I played right field and caught every ball hit to me. That was the only reason I was on the team; I was one of the best outfielders in the league.

"Mom, do you know where my sneakers are?" I asked from upstairs.

"Check under your bed. Better hurry up, Willy, or you'll be late for your game."

That's where they were. *I don't know how it is, but mothers seem to know where things are when you don't have a clue. They just have this mysterious power of knowing.*

"How do I look, Mom?"

"Like a professional baseball player—straighten your cap."

"You and dad coming to the game?"

"After supper. Wanna ride to the town hall?"

"I'll take my bike."

"Aren't you gonna kiss me for good luck?" my mother asked while she removed her apron and shut off the burner on the stove.

I quickly kissed her on the cheek, grabbed my glove, and then headed for the front door.

"Willy?"

"Yeah, Mom?"

"Knock it out of the park."

I rolled my eyes and left for the game.

At the bottom of the ninth inning, the score was 8 to 6, in the other team's favor. We were at bat. In the prior innings, I struck out three times, walked once, and scored a run. There was one out, one man on first, one on second. Jimmy Dee, our pitcher was at bat; I was on deck. Jimmy had three balls and two strikes on him. Kevin Lee wound up and flung a high fast ball that almost went wild. Ball four. Jimmy walked to first, and the bases were loaded. *Shit!* Just then the park lights illuminated the baseball diamond while I reluctantly approached the batter's box. I wiped the sweat off my palms, clenched my favorite bat, and then tapped home plate with it.

From the outfield, I heard someone yell, "here comes the strikeout king!"

In the other team's dugout, everyone clapped and chanted: "Willy Willy Willy Willy Willy Willy Willy."

The Tiger's coach quieted the team, and he called a time-out. With a slight limp and his head down, the coach meandered to the pitcher's mound and signaled for his star relief pitcher, Jake Voltary, a lefty, to relieve Mr. Lee, who dejectedly banged his glove with his fist and walked off the field.

I stepped out of the batter's box while the new pitcher made a few warm-up throws.

Before he returned the protective mask to his face, Jimmy Doulin, the home plate umpire, shouted, "play ball!"

I took a deep breath and calmly eyed the pitcher while he briefly glanced at the runner on first base. He shot a fastball for a strike. I never saw it go by me. *Maybe mom was right about wearing glasses.*

I stepped back, wiped the perspiration off my brow, and then suddenly heard the other team's mocking banter again. Only this time, it sounded like a loud whisper. Even some people in the bleachers were saying it. "Willy Willy Willy Willy Willy Willy . . ."

Like my ability to astral travel, I was also born with the power to block out sound. I used it then. The only thing I heard were my mother's words before I left the house for the game. *Knock it out of the park, Willy.*

Jake Voltary threw another pitch, a knuckle ball this time.

I said to myself, *How the hell am I supposed to knock it out of the park when I can't even see it.*

"Strike two!" the umpire bellowed.

Someone yelled from the stands, "loser!"

A voice in my head told me a curve ball would come next. The lefty vigorously rubbed the ball, went into his wind-up, and the sphere left his hand. Sure enough, the pitch curved, and it hung in front of me like the moon I saw last night. I swung all my might, hit the ball, and it rocketed past the pitcher's head and over the center field fence.

I recognized my mother's loud voice from the bleachers: "Way to go, Willy!"

A grand slam homerun. It felt like a dream as I trotted around the bases and reached home plate. Everyone at the ballpark, including my team, was in shock. Jake Voltary (the relief pitcher) was sobbing like a baby. His parents were too. We won. Ten to eight.

And that was the last baseball game I ever played.

Chapter 4

My father bragged all week about me to all his steady customers in the deli; although some people said it was absolute luck I hit a grand slam home run. My mother and I knew it was way more than that: *she believed it was a miracle.*

That Summer, I participated in one last apple fight in the orchard by the baseball field at the town hall. While the angry farmer chased us out of the orchard, I had to climb the chain link fence in a hurry; in the process, my hand got caught on a barb on the top; my skin ripped open, and I dropped to the ground to safety. I looked at my hand, and it wasn't bleeding.

That fall, I entered South Junior High, blinked my eyes, and then I was a high school freshman sitting at a desk in homeroom, at Newburgh Free Academy. I joined the school band and orchestra. And became more serious about pursuing a career as a musician. Countless days and nights while I attended 10th through 12th grade, I stayed after school and practiced my clarinet for six hours straight. The janitor, or security guard would have to unlock the school door to let me out. I'd ride my bike home. Some days, I cut class, set up my music stand, and practiced for hours in Downing Park.

In the spring of 74', my parents gave me a brand-new clarinet for my high school graduation.

I started taking the train from Beacon into Manhattan, pounding the sidewalks on Broadway two days a week. I put in applications and talked to orchestra managers who might need a clarinet player. I did that for four months, until I finally found a gig two nights a week in the theater district, playing in an orchestra for a Broadway musical: *Fiddler on the Roof.*

My mom and dad were thrilled. *Guess all those long hours studying music paid off.*

After two years with the Broadway company, I managed to work my way up to second-chair clarinetist.

Five years later, in the Summer of '81, after an evening performance of the *Fiddler,* I was relaxing backstage, when a well-dressed gentleman approached me. He wore a navy-blue suit, and was humming a tune from the show: *Sunrise Sunset.* He had a glossy bald head, and a wide grin.

"Hi, my name is Lou Lewison. I'm the manager of the Amsterdam Philharmonic Orchestra."

"Willy Maze. It's nice to meet you, Mr. Lewison."

"Likewise. I always wanted to see *Fiddler on the Roof*. I finally got the chance. I'm a huge fan of Jerrold Bock."

"Yeah, he's a great composer. So, what's your official critique of the show?"

"Phenomenal. Can I buy you dinner somewhere, Mr. Maze? I'd like to speak to you about our orchestra. One of our clarinetists will be leaving in the near future. Someone with your talent could definitely be a plus for our company."

"I know a place off Broadway," I told the gentleman. "It's called Sardi's."

That evening, Mr. Lou Lewison and I discussed the second-chair clarinetist position for the Amsterdam Philharmonic. Over some cognac and tiramisu, I signed a three-year contract with the orchestra, and we sealed the deal with an espresso and a handshake. That worked out well for me, because my contract with the *Fiddler* musical would end the following month. Besides, I needed a change from playing the same old music night after night for the last seven years.

In August of '81, I said goodbye to my parents and boarded a 747. The iron bird left Newburgh, and I sadly watched the mystical green hills of the Hudson Valley fade in the distance. As I listened to some Chet Baker through headphones, the jet passed over the rippling waves of the Atlantic, and into the darkness.

Chapter 5

The orchestra manager met me outside the KLM terminal in Amsterdam, where I packed my bags into his cardinal red Porsch, and he drove to the centrum of Amsterdam. Mr. Lewison had arranged for me to rent a $300 a month furnished one-bedroom apartment on a street called the Museumplein, two blocks from the Van Gogh Art Museum, and opposite a popular Indian restaurant called Yogananda's Curry House, owned by a Pakistani man named Babu and his wife, Indira; he was also the proprietor of a coffee shop in the back.

The apartment was on the second floor of a three-story brick building built in 1785. Two steel gargoyles angrily glanced down from the roof when we arrived.

"Here we are, Mr. Maze," the orchestra manager announced as he parked his sports car.

I got out and viewed a peculiar sculpture garden in the front of the apartment building. One of the sculptures was a brown and white metal object with ornamental shapes curved from its base to the top. Another work of art which sat on a triangular metal base, was a replica of a reddish tan pyramid two feet high. Colored a grayish blue, a large glass diamond was balanced on the top of the geometric object.

"Modern art," the orchestra manager mentioned.

"It's clever. Is this the place?"

"Yes, I'll help you with your things."

Mr. Lewison opened the trunk, and we carried my baggage into the Baroque-style building.

"Mrs. Vanderkughel, the landlady, lives on the third floor. She's a bit eccentric. You'll meet her shortly. One of our oboe players in the orchestra occupies the first floor flat. Are you allergic to birds by any chance?"

"No, why?"

"She has a noisy parrot and a love bird."

"The oboist?"

"Yes."

"No, I'm not allergic to birds."

The place felt haunted to me as we climbed the steps to the second floor and walked through an open doorway.

"We're here, Mrs. Vanderkughel," Mr. Lewison announced.

"I'm in the kitchen," a woman called.

We went down a hallway, and I saw a middle-aged woman seated at a kitchen table with a pen and papers in front of her. Judging by her work clothes, she looked as if she recently did some house cleaning.

"*Goedemorgen*, gentlemen," the landlord greeted in Dutch.

"Good morning, Mrs. Vanderkughel. This is your new tenant, Mr. William Maze. He's from New York. He'll be playing in the orchestra with us."

"What instrument do you play, Mr. Maze?—I hope it's not the fucking tuba—like my last tenant played. He made too much noise."

"I play the clarinet, Mrs. Kugel."

"It's pronounced Vanderkughel."

"Sorry."

"Well, I must be on my way," the orchestra manager said. "And don't forget, Willy. Rehearsal is at two o'clock tomorrow."

"Thanks for your help, Mr. Lewison."

"No problem. Enjoy your new home."

The landlady gave me a tour of the flat, and we sat at the kitchen table, where I filled out the rental agreement.

"Will you be needing a telephone, Mr. Maze?"

"Yes. You can call me Willy."

"I'll contact the phone company today and have them connect the number in your name. You'll get a call from them in the morning."

"Yes, ma'am."

I finished filling out the form and signed it while the landlord went over her rules and regulations:

"I don't allow subletting, no wild parties, no loud music after 8 pm, no smoking weed or tobacco in the apartment. And no cats, dogs, or reptiles."

"I understand."

"I hope you do."

I shook hands with my new landlady, and she got off her chair to leave.

"Oh . . . I almost forgot. There's one more important rule I expect you to follow while you're here."

"What's that?"

"The basement is strictly off limits to tenants and guests. I don't allow anyone to go down there for any reason whatsoever. That includes the storage of boxes, bicycles, furniture, or anything else."

"Of course, Mrs. Vanderkughel."

"Good."

After a three-hour nap, I opened the curtains in the living room and saw that it was dark out. I dressed, locked the door to the flat, and then went downstairs to get something to eat at the restaurant across the street. Before I left the building, I thought about what the landlady said regarding the basement. I noticed a door across from the apartment on the first floor. *Maybe it leads to the cellar. What's in there that's so taboo?* I asked myself.

I stood in front of the door, grasped the round black knob, and then turned it.

I heard a door creak open behind me.

"What are you doing?"

I quickly let go of the doorknob and turned around to face a tall, slender, fair-skinned young woman with uncommonly large lips. She was barefoot, wore jeans, and a man's white t-shirt with no bra underneath it. A blue and yellow feathered parrot was perched on her shoulder; it repeated her question: *"What are you doing?"*

"I just moved into the apartment upstairs—hi, I'm Willy."

"Hi, I'm Willy," the bird repeated.

I offered the woman my hand.

"Lotty Lipshitz. My parrot's name is Rembrandt."

"My name is Rembrandt," the well-spoken creature cackled from its owner's shoulder.

"Mrs. Vanderkughel didn't tell you the basement was off-limits?"

"She did, but I was curious."

"Curiosity killed the cat," the parrot stated.

"Quiet, Rembrandt."

"Mr. Lewison told me that you play the oboe."

"That's right. You?"

"Clarinet. I was just about to grab a bite at the Indian place. How's the food there?"

"It's excellent," the semi-dressed woman replied. "I'm hungry also. I'll put Rembrandt inside, and we can go."

Moments later, Lotty came out of her flat wearing a gray sweatshirt and clogs. We walked over to the restaurant.

On the front window of Yogananda's was a picture of a chef in whites, standing on his head. An Indian woman with an exceptionally long nose greeted us at the hostess station, and we were seated at a table covered with a red and white tablecloth. I was amazed how lengthy the hostess's nose was. We opened our menus.

I observed Lotty's unusually large and well-defined lips.

"What are you looking at?" the oboist inquired while glancing up from the menu.

"Your embouchure. I would think you need good lip and tongue control to play the oboe."

"I guess. How long have you played the clarinet?"

"Since the third grade. Where you from, Lotty?"

"Antwerp, Belgium. You?"

"Upstate New York."

Dressed in a white shirt and red necktie, an Indian waiter appeared at our table, "Are we ready to order, Ms. Lipshitz?"

After we ate, the owner's wife {the chef} came out to our table and asked us how we liked our food. She wore curry-stained chef's whites, had a bright red dot on her forehead, a tall gold chef's hat, and a nose that was reminiscent of an elephant's trunk. We told her everything was delicious. We paid separate checks, and Lotty suggested we have dessert and coffee at Baba's Coffee Shop in the back.

The menu didn't look like it had the kind of selections a coffee shop in New York would have. One page listed the types of hashish they offered: Moroccan Brown, Nepalese Temple Balls, Afghani Black, and Indian Red. The page opposite listed the varieties of marijuana: Super Skunk, Maui Wowie, Afghan Kush, Acapulco Gold, and Purple Haze.

"I don't smoke pot, Lotty. Never have."

"Me either. I usually get their space cake. Or the brownies infused with high potency THC."

"How are they?"

"Pretty good."

A Pakistani man approached our table and greeted us.

"Good evening, Ms. Lipshitz. So nice to see you again. And you brought a friend. Welcome."

"Thank you."

"This is Willy, Baba. He's new in the orchestra."

"Very good," the Pakistani man said. "What are we having tonight?"

"I'll take a cappuccino and a double chocolate brownie, please," the woman replied. "No whipped cream."

"And for you, sir?"

"A green tea and a space cake."

"With or without whipped cream?"

"With."

Baba smiled, bowed, and simply said, *very good.*

When Lotty and I left the coffee shop, it felt as if I was walking on air; the two glasses of wine, and the space cake, had given me a rather good buzz. I hovered across the street, slipped inside the gargoyle protected apartment building, and then I bid my first-floor neighbor a goodnight. I tumbled up the staircase, unlocked my front door, and then crashed on the red leather couch in the living room.

Chapter 6

While a diaphanous orange radiance filtered in from behind the living room curtains, I rubbed the grit from my eyes and lounged on the couch a few minutes before finding some ground coffee and filters in the kitchen cupboard. I poured water into a Mister Coffee machine, showered, and then dressed.

The night before, my neighbor and I planned on going to rehearsal together, so I drank another cup of coffee while leafing through some music Mr. Lewison had given me yesterday, and by midday, I left the apartment with my clarinet, went downstairs, and then knocked on my neighbor's door. Yikes! I don't know if she meant to grab my attention, or not, but it did; when the tall woman opened the door, she was wearing a pair of tight jeans, high black boots, and absolutely nothing on top. She nonchalantly smiled and turned around.

"Good afternoon, Willy. Come on in, I have to finish putting on my makeup," she said while walking to the bathroom. "I had fun last night."

"Me too," I said, checking out the birds.

"Are you ready for your first rehearsal?"

"I believe so."

The parrot was eating, while the love bird was sitting on its perch and heatedly whistling. That's not all it was doing. The yellow creature was rubbing against a small wooden pole and turning itself on. Lotty came out to the living room fully dressed, in high boots, a black derby over her short mop of bright brown hair—like she was going horseback riding.

"That's Maxine. Don't mind her—she's just horny— have you eaten lunch yet, Willy?"

"Only coffee and some pastries."

"We can grab something on the way—I'm ready."

"She's just horny," the bird copied.

After eating sandwiches, we caught the tram to the Concertgebouw, a historic building where the rehearsal was located. Lotty informed me the architecture was amazing, inside, and out, and the hall had some of the best acoustics in the world.

We got off the tram and walked a short way to our destination. While I stopped to admire the decorative front facade of the Concertgebouw, the oboe player stood face to face with me, puckered her unusually large lips, and then planted a kiss on mine.

I asked somewhat surprised: "What was that for?"

"It's good luck to kiss at the entrance. An old tradition that dates back to the time of Mozart."

"Really?"

"Come on, Willy. You don't wanna be late for your first rehearsal."

I found my seat in the clarinet section next to the first-chair clarinetist, an older, balding gentleman in a blue dress shirt, yellow sports jacket, black slacks, and wing-tip shoes. He was a little on the mismatched side in my opinion. We introduced ourselves. His name was almost as strange as his outfit: Woodrow Herman. I wondered if his nickname was Woody, like the famous jazz clarinetist, Woody Herman.

I opened my clarinet case, put together my instrument, and then blew some notes as the conductor arrived. Mr. Sonata. The five-foot, one-inch Japanese man climbed the steps of a two-foot wooden pedestal, and he stood by his music stand and tapped it with a baton. The hall went silent. When everyone was in their respective sections, the little conductor announced: "I'm happy to introduce and welcome a new member to our woodwind section. Second chair clarinetist from New York. Please give a warm welcome to Mr. William Maze. Please stand Mr. Maze."

With my instrument in hand, I proudly stood, smiled, and then bowed my head while the orchestra members applauded. I sat, we tuned, and then practiced for three hours, with a bathroom and coffee break in between compositions by Beethoven, Tchaikovsky, Chopin, Vivaldi, and Debussy. And that concluded my first rehearsal with the Amsterdam Philharmonic Orchestra.

Chapter 7

The next two weeks, the oboe player's kisses had become more fervent in front of the concert hall. She and I would have coffee some mornings, and meet for dinner at the Indian restaurant three nights a week. Afterward, we would indulge in various mind-expanding edibles at Baba's Coffeeshop. I became a regular there.

On one particular occasion at Baba's, Lotty and I decided to order a couple of hash brownies and space cakes to go. She invited me back to her place to share a bottle of cognac. The conductor had granted the orchestra a much-needed two-day rest before we were to do a series of concerts at the Concertgebouw.

"Take off your shoes and make yourself comfortable, Willy. I'll get some glasses down."

"Make yourself comfortable, Willy," the parrot annoyingly repeated. "I'll get some glasses down."

"I'd like to go to the Van Gogh Museum tomorrow. Are you free?" I asked while unlacing my sneakers.

"Are you free?" the bird cawed.

"That's enough Rembrandt—eat your dinner. I have to get a pedicure in the morning—we could go sometime in the afternoon."

"That sounds good."

"Here's to your success in the orchestra," the large-lipped oboist toasted.

"To success."

We knocked our glasses together and the velvety liquid dribbled down my throat. It was the second week of September, and it felt cool and damp outside. The wonderful thing about Lotty's apartment—I didn't have—was the stone fireplace. Eduardo, a Spanish, barrel-chested tuba player had provided her with some firewood. She must have read my mind.

"Why don't you get a fire going, Willy. There's a lighter on the mantlepiece."

"I'm all for that."

I crumpled up newspaper, placed kindling and split wood on top, and then started a flame.

After some cognac and a couple space cakes, my neighbor kindled one herself. She seductively moved her long white fingers up my leg, and dangerously approached my groin area. She stuck her wet tongue in my ear.

"You like that?"

"Yeah."

"Do you want me to stop?"

"No. But I have to tell you something very personal, Lotty."

"What's that?"

"I've never had sex with a woman before."

"Why—are you queer?"

"No, I'm a virgin."

Rembrandt ruffled his feathers, elongated his neck, and then repeated in a singsong manner: "Like a virgin. Make yourself comfortable, Willy. I'll get some glasses down."

"Shut up, Rembrandt. He loves Madonna's music. How old are you, Willy?"

"I just turned twenty-five."

"And you're still a virgin? When's your birthday?"

"It was yesterday."

"Serious?"

"Yeah."

"Well, happy belated birthday!"

"Thank you."

"I'm seven years older than you," Lotty stated.

"And I'm guessing you're not a virgin."

"No, I'm not. Now we really have to celebrate," she said as she released me, reached for the bottle, and then poured more cognac into our glasses. "Here's to you, Willy."

"Cheers."

"Do you want your birthday present now or later?"

"I'll take it now."

"Wait here."

I munched on a space cake while the lanky woman got up from the couch, went inside her bedroom, the bathroom, and then ten minutes later: she came out wearing a red silk kimono, a patchouli scented perfume, fresh lipstick, and black heels. She stood in front of me and inquired:

"How do you like your birthday present?"

"It's really nice. I mean you look nice."

"Thank you."

Lotty and I slept very little that night. And she cancelled her pedicure appointment the next day. We never went to the Van Gogh Museum that afternoon either. And in my wildest dreams, I never imagined I would lose my virginity to a 5'9" Belgian woman who played the oboe, had a talkative parrot and a horny love bird. Two days later, I bumped into my landlady on the stairwell.

"Nice to see you, Mrs. Vanderkughel."

"What the fuck was all that loud noise about the other night, Mr. Maze? It sounded like someone was having a multiple orgasm. It was coming from Lotty's apartment."

"Maybe it was her parrot. I didn't hear anything, Mrs. Vanderkughel. I wear earplugs when I sleep. And I'm a really heavy sleeper."

"You know what the rules are around here, Mr. Maze."

"Yes, Mrs. Vanderkughel. I do."

Chapter 8

After touring the Anne Frank House on the Prisengracht, I purchased some groceries at a small market, returned to my apartment on the Museumplein, and then sat on the red leather couch in the living room. The phone rang. My mother's voice come through the receiver of a black, antiquated rotary phone.

"Willy?"

"Hi Mom. How's everything?"

"Fine. We received your postcard three weeks ago. Thanks. Did you get your birthday card?"

"It came today. Thank you."

"How's the orchestra?"

"So far so good. I'm learning the ropes as they say. I met a girl. I mean a woman. She lives downstairs from me. She has a parrot. And a love bird."

"A parrot?"

"Yeah, that's what I said. Her name is Lotty."

"She has a parrot named Lotty?"

"No, Mom. My neighbor's name is Lotty. She plays the oboe in the orchestra."

"Is she Jewish?"

"Half."

"Harry—Willy met a nice Jewish girl—she plays in the orchestra with him."

"Terrific. It's about time," I heard my father say in the background.

"The orchestra is going on a tour soon, Mom. Starting in November."

"Where to?"

"The United States and South America. We'll be performing a couple shows at Lincoln Center and Carnegie Hall. I'll get tickets for you and Dad. I believe those concerts are scheduled for the end of November. Beginning of December. I'll call and let you know."

"I'm proud of you, Willy. Here, say hello to your father."

"Hi, Dad. How's it going?"

"Hello, William. I'm okay. Newburgh hasn't changed much since you left. Same old crap, different day. How's life in Amsterdam?"

"I love it here. I have a girlfriend now."

"I heard," my father said. "How'd that come about? You've never had a girlfriend in your life, Willy."

"That's because I've been so occupied with music, Dad."

"How's the weather in Amsterdam?"

"A little rainy and cool. Well, I have to get ready for rehearsal. It was nice talking to you. Love you."

"Love you too, son. Here's your mother again."

"So, let me know when you're coming to New York, Willy. And don't smoke any grass over there."

"Mom, you know I don't smoke pot. Love you."

After rehearsal, I stopped at a little place and ate some French fries smothered in warm peanut sauce. A Dutch delicacy. Afterward, I rode the tram to the Museumplein, walked to my building, and then noticed Lotty's little blue bicycle was gone from the spot near the sculpture garden, where she always kept it unlocked. *She must have gone for a ride.* I went inside, knocked on her door but there was nobody home except for Rembrandt and Maxine. I heard the parrot inside squawk, "Who is it?"

Damn bird doesn't miss a trick. The other night while making love to Lotty, I could have sworn I heard the parrot say once or twice: "Don't stop, Eduardo." *I wonder what that was all about.*

I looked across the hall at the cellar door and noticed that it was partially ajar, and a light was on. I opened the door all the way and observed a luminous yellow staircase that descended a long way until the bottom. I called from the top step:

"Is someone down there?" *I suppose the landlady forgot to close it.* I darkened the light, shut the cellar door, and moments after, Mrs. Vanderkughel came out of her apartment. Our paths crossed at the second-floor landing.

"Hello, Willy."

"Hi, Mrs. Vanderkughel."

"Something wrong? You seem a bit flustered."

"No, ma'am. Just exhausted from a long rehearsal."

"Need anything for the apartment? —I'm off to the hardware store for some household items."

"No there isn't, thanks. Have a good afternoon."

"You as well, Willy."

That was close, I thought.

I went inside, heated some water, and then made myself an extra potent chamomile tea with honey and lemon. I drank it and finished off a pot brownie.

Now, I was really curious about the basement. I thought it would be a perfect opportunity to do some astral traveling. *Why not the cellar? Perhaps it wouldn't be a good idea. Oh, why not. The landlady wouldn't even know I was down there in my invisible astral body. And she'll be gone for a while anyway.*

I reclined on the couch, closed my eyes, and then imagined the cellar door and the stairs leading into the forbidden basement. Feeling a weightlessness, my astral body transcended four feet above, and I viewed my mortal body on the couch. Moments later, I was on the first floor, opening the cellar door, and turning on the light.

Chapter 9

At the bottom of the airy yellow staircase, I discovered a varied collection of dust covered musical instruments under two naked lightbulbs: a couple of violins, a French horn, a spider-webbed harp, a dented trumpet, piano, and various drums and other percussion instruments. I picked up a mallet and struck a large brass gong. The sound reverberated throughout the cellar and up into the hallway.

"Hey—not so loud—you'll wake the dead," someone in the basement announced.

Startled, I turned to see who had spoken; a frosty-whiskered figure with a transparent white face, and a body with the same make up. Similar apparitions appeared, and they started playing the musical instruments.

"Who are you?"

"Willy. I just moved into the apartment on the second floor."

"Hi, I'm Mikhail. Looks like you've got them up."

"Who?"

"The other ghosts. We live down here."

"Why?"

"We have to be somewhere. You must be new in town."

"I am. But I'm not a ghost."

"You play in the orchestra?" the ghost inquired.

"Yeah, the clarinet. Second chair."

Mikhail smoothly ran a stick along the bars of a xylophone.

"I played in the same orchestra 15 years ago," the ghost stated. "I lived in the apartment on the first floor. Loved the fireplace. Warmer than down here. Who lives there now?"

"A woman named Lotty. She plays the oboe."

"She have a noisy parrot?"

"Yeah."

"Sometimes I hear it at night."

"How'd you die?" I asked the ghost.

"I owed a lot of money to people I shouldn't have borrowed from. I couldn't pay them back, so they broke my arms and legs and threw me into the North Sea."

"I'm sorry about that."

"That's life. My own fault. I shouldn't have gone to the red-light district so often. Temptation got the best of me."

"What's the red-light district?" I asked.

"You are new in town," the ghost said. "It's a place where the red lights are aglow, day and night, rain or shine. Some of the most beautiful women on earth sit almost naked inside, behind undraped windows, for anyone to see. They offer their bodies in exchange for money. What man wouldn't be tempted?"

"They're prostitutes?"

"Yeah. Much of the money I earned playing in the orchestra was spent on them. That, and smoking grass. I could hardly pay my rent. I borrowed from loan sharks. And was eaten by real sharks."

"Why are all these musical instruments down here?"

"They belong to Mrs. Vanderkughel. They were once owned by former members of the orchestra who used to live in the apartments above. Like me, those former tenants weren't able to pay their rent, so the landlord took their instruments in lieu of money."

So that's why the landlord doesn't allow anyone in the cellar. "Where's the red-light district?"

"Through that door," Mikhail replied. "I could show you—you could have any woman you want there. Black, brown, white, tall, short, petite, skinny, fat, small tits, buxom, blonde, brunette, blue-eyed, short hair, long hair. What do you say?"

"Okay. Take me there."

"Don't listen to him, Willy," a feminine sounding voice warned from the top of the cellar stairs. "He's not real. It's only a temptation speaking."

I couldn't hear the warning, because of the ghost orchestra's cacophonous music.

Mikhail and I went down a long, steep, white-washed incline, brightly lit, and colder the farther we went. I saw red lights, windows, and doors. Behind the windows sat skimpily dressed flirting figures beckoning me with boney fingers.

"This is the red-light district, Willy. Have yourself a good time."

He laughed.

"They're only skeletons," I said while Mikhail laughed some more.

As I watched the macabre scene, the ghost vanished into thin air. I went farther down the incline, and into a world more submerged. An underground Amsterdam, where an extraordinarily large room was filled with gruesome, fur-covered men and women with horns. They smoked, snorted, and drank intoxicants at a long bar. Some danced to ear splitting music. Others ran naked, participating in wild, sadistic orgies on the cold white floor. Other hair-covered demons played gambling games, cards, and slot machines.

When one of the horned men saw me in my astral body, the room became quiet.

"Who is this? He's not from this purgatory," one of them said.

"No—he has a soul—he must be from the upper world."

"Yes—and if we capture him—we can find our way out of here," someone else spoke.

I tried leaving the demon-filled party, but it was too late, because one of the horned beings had taken an empty glass jar and caught my astral body in it like a firefly. A napkin was placed over the opening and secured with a rubber band; I was trapped inside. They placed the glass with me in it, on a shelf in the bar for safekeeping. I flew around inside, futilely bumping into the glass. Every now and then, a bartender came up to the jar, tapped on it and turned their nose up at me.

Grotesquely thick steaks were cooked bloody rare and brought out and eaten. With their bellies full, the red-complexioned demons grew tired and fell asleep on the floor.

From inside the jar, I watched a large moth fly around the room, land by the bar in front of me, where it morphed into an adult-size woman with a face and large wings. It wasn't a woman though, but the guardian spirit I met in Woodstock. She released the rubber band, removed the napkin from the jar, and then my astral body flew out.

"Chakra!"

"You were told not to go into the cellar, Willy."

"I know— but I wanted to see what was here."

"What's down here is *Purgatory*. Follow me out."

My guardian spirit's brightly colored wheels of light guided my astral body up the pitch-black incline, and into the basement cluttered with musical instruments.

"Don't come down here ever again, Willy. Or you'll never be able to leave," my guardian spirit warned.

Before departing the gruesome netherworld, I briefly listened to a headless pianist walk his spectral fingers along some broken ivory keys.

I shut the basement door, floated up the stairs to my apartment, and then merged with my physical body that was reclining on the sofa.

Chapter 10

On the 9th of November, the orchestra began a five-week tour of major cities in South America and the United States. Our first concert was in Buenos Aires, then São Paulo, Lima, and Rio. After that, we had performances in Los Angeles, San Fran, Houston, Dallas, Atlanta, Miami, New Orleans, Philly, Boston, and New York.

We played our last concert at Carnegie Hall. I got front-row tickets for my mom and dad, and booked them a room at The Waldorf Astoria, the luxurious hotel, where me and most of the other musicians were registered. I was excited to see them, and they were thrilled to have attended our last performance of the tour.

After the show, I invited my parents backstage to meet Lotty, and the four of us had supper at the famous Stage Deli, before heading back to the hotel. The next morning, my mom and dad went home while we stayed an extra day to sightsee and take in a Broadway show: *The Phantom of the Opera*.

A day later, Lotty and I checked out of the Waldorf and drove a rental car upstate, leisurely cruising the scenic Palisades Parkway north, onto Route 87, and into a quiet town of Newburgh. While night fell, I hit Union Avenue, drove down the hill past Epiphany College, and then pulled into my parent's driveway on Oak Street. We got out and carried some gifts to the front door. I rang the bell, and my mother appeared.

"Hi Mom."

"Willy, Lotty! Come in."

"Hi, Mrs. Maze. It's nice to see you again."

"We got you and dad some gifts from the city."

"You shouldn't have. Willy and Lotty are here, Harry."

"Welcome, Lotty," my father enthusiastically greeted, barely paying attention to me. Make yourself at home. Let me take your coat, sweetheart."

"Thank you, Mr. Maze."

"Terrific."

"Hello, Willy."

"Hi, Dad."

"Etta, make some fresh coffee."

"I already have, Harry."

"Would you like a coffee?" my father asked while he escorted Lotty over to the couch where he always sat.

"Yes, please."

After I used the toilet upstairs, I came down and rested on the armchair near the picture window; the thick plastic still protected the gold velvet seat like it had since my father purchased it 20 years ago.

"Do you take cream or sugar, Lotty?"

"Just black, Mrs. Maze."

My father immediately warmed up to the oboe player *as if she was his girlfriend.* Somewhat annoyed, my mother put on her jacket and smoked a cigarette on the front porch.

"My wife tells me you're from Belgium, Lotty."

"That's right, Mr. Maze. Antwerp."

My mother came back inside the house and poured herself a coffee.

"I thought you quit smoking, Mom."

"I stopped for a while. Leave me alone."

"Sorry."

My father gently squeezed Lotty's forearm and had himself a good sniff of her perfume. He told her one of his corny jokes. And she laughed.

"Where are you performing next, sweetheart? Maybe we can come and hear you."

"Our next tour dates won't be until Christmas, Mr. Maze."

"Where?"

"Italy."

"I never been to Italy. Maybe we should go, Etta."

"Keep dreaming Harry. We can't afford to travel. What do you have scheduled after Italy."

"China, Japan, Taiwan and Singapore," I replied.

"My son, the traveling musician. He reminds me of the wandering Jews in the bible. You need to settle down already, Willy. Maybe raise a family. When are you and Lotty getting married?"

"We're not even engaged, Dad."

"Oh."

I could tell our conversation was making Lotty a bit uncomfortable.

"Oh, leave him alone, Harry," my mother said. "He's happy. That's all that matters. Anyone wanna piece of chocolate cake?"

"No cake, Mrs. Maze. I'm on a gluten-free and sugar-free diet."

"I'll have a piece, Mom."

While my mother went to the kitchen to cut a slice of cake, my father put his hand on my girlfriend's knee. "You know, Lotty. My wife has a cousin who's gluten-free. He came to visit a couple of years ago. When nobody knew what gluten-free was. How 'bout that?"

"Really?" Lotty asked with a brief laugh.

"Her cousin had hair down to his back, a long beard, and he always dressed in white."

"My cousin has a name, Harry," my mother said as she handed me a plate and fork.

"What's his name, Etta?"

"Sonny, dear."

"That's right. Her cousin Sonny was a gluten-free vegetarian. He only ate tofu and bean sprouts while he was here. And did yoga and meditated every day. *Incidental* meditation."

"I think you mean transcendental meditation, Dad."

"Whatever. Are you sure you don't want any cake, Lotty? Maybe a nice lean corned beef sandwich on rye from my deli. Or some Ben and Jerry's ice cream? Get Lotty some ice cream, Willy."

"Harry, stop it," my mother admonished.

"I was just trying to be hospitable."

"We had a big dinner earlier," my girlfriend mentioned. "And I don't eat meat, or food with white sugar in it anymore."

"I don't either. I'm a diabetic."

"That's too bad, Mr. Maze."

"We loved the performance the other night, Lotty," my mother said.

"Thank you, Mrs. Maze."

Dad told my girlfriend another joke while mom opened the gifts we brought: souvenirs from the World Trade Center, the Statue of Liberty, a purple necktie from Macys, and two coffee mugs from the Carnegie Hall gift shop.

"Thanks for the gifts, Willy."

"You're welcome. We're gonna head up to the bed and breakfast soon. Lotty and I are exhausted."

"You coming over for lunch tomorrow, Willy?"

"What time, Mom?"

"Twelve is good."

"Great. You ready to go, Lotty?"

At the Hungry Bear bed and breakfast tucked away in the woods, four miles from downtown New Paltz, my girlfriend and I listened to the frogs sing by the pond in the back yard while we steeped in a hot tub, enjoying a glass of wine underneath a million stars.

Chapter 11

After Lotty and I enjoyed a delightful gluten-free lunch at mom and dad's, we travelled south, passed West Point and then entered Bear Mountain State Park. I turned and turned up a steep and winding road to the summit and parked. She and I walked over to where some jagged grey cliffs met the stark blue sky. One false step meant a long plummet to the bottom, where a timeless green Hudson River flowed into a midmorning sun. I watched a bald eagle circle above, envisioning the Indian spirit who had spoken to me in the park. I felt a strong spiritual connection in the place we stood.

We got in the car, and I drove south toward the city. After dropping the rental car off at Kennedy International, Lotty and I flew nonstop to Europe. Eight hours later, we retrieved our bags in the KLM terminal.

She got on a flight to Belgium to visit her sister in Antwerp while I took the train into Amsterdam.

When I arrived at Central Station it was cold, dark, and deserted; there were no taxis or trams in sight, so I hoofed the quarter mile back to my apartment. My breath formed clouds as I exhaled along the station promenade, holding my clarinet case, tuxedo, and rolling the suitcase a distance.

I paused to rest near a window with a glowing red light above it. Inside, a hooker was seductively perched on a stool with her pale legs crossed; she was dressed in a black lace bra and matching underpants. I observed her tempting figure for a few moments while she smiled at me and cupped her hands over her breasts.

I proceeded home along a cobblestone walking street. After a few minutes, I heard the tapping of footsteps behind me; I stopped, turned around, and saw two unfriendly looking men dressed in long gray coats; hats partially covered their eyes. One man held out a cigarette and gestured for a light while the other man punched me in the forehead with a razor-sharp object between his knuckles.

My skin was punctured, and the object deeply penetrated my skull. I bled. Profusely. One of them grabbed the handle of my clarinet case and tried to pull it away from me. I screamed while blood ran down my face and onto a white shirt and brown sports jacket. Inside a bar nearby, someone heard my desperate screams above a blaring jukebox, and a patron came out of the tavern and scared the hoodlums away. I dropped the clarinet case, and it bounced twice on the hard cobblestone. Warm, thick blood obscured my vision while the criminals scampered up the walking street.

I rested on my back and pressed a hand over the gash. A woman appeared, and she unsparingly doused my forehead with the contents of a liquor bottle. A commotion of people gathered around me while an ambulance siren wailed.

I spoke to someone from my subconscious:

"Who are you?"

"Your guardian spirit."

"Am I dead?"

"No, Willy. You're not dead. Just badly hurt."

"Where am I?"

"You're in a hospital room. You'll be fine. Go back inside your body and heal."

I gained consciousness while a doctor applied a butterfly bandage to my injured skin; he stuck my arm with a Tetanus shot and introduced himself.

"Hi, I'm Dr. Princengracht."

"Hello."

I put a hand up to block the harsh light above my head.

"How bad is it? How many stitches?"

"It's a deep wound, but the skin is too thin to stitch in that area," the emergency room doctor answered. "It's a miracle your eye wasn't cut. I believe you suffered a minor concussion though. What instrument do you play, Mr. Maze?"

"What?" I asked.

"Do you play music?"

I had to think for a moment. I saw my instrument case near the rest of my things.

"I play the clarinet."

"I thought so. I recognized you from one of the concerts I attended at the Concertgebouw," the doctor said while he gave me a bottle of pills. "It's for the pain. Two every six hours."

"Can I leave now?"

"Yes, but I would take it easy for a week," the doctor replied. "Ice your head for a couple days. And no strenuous physical activity."

"What about the bill?" I asked.

"Your insurance covered everything."

"Great. Thanks for your help, doctor."

"You're welcome. I'll call a cab for you now."

The day after the mugging, the pain was so excruciating, I had difficulty getting out of bed. I called the orchestra manager.

"Hello."

"Mr. Lewison, it's Willy Maze."

"What's up, Willy?"

"I had a little accident."

"What happened? You sound terrible."

"Two guys attacked me after I came back from the airport last night. I was stabbed in the forehead."

"Oh my God—they steal anything—are you okay?"

"Nothing was stolen, but I lost a little blood. I'll be out of commission for a while. I fucking hurt like hell, Lou."

"Is Lotty all right?" the orchestra manager asked.

"She wasn't with me."

"Just relax, Willy. Take some time off and recuperate. We don't have any concerts until Christmas."

Lotty came home two days later, and she called me up and I told her what happened. She came to visit and brought me some food from the Indian restaurant. The day after, my landlady showed up at my door with a container in her hands.

"Hi, Mrs. Vanderkughel."

"Hi Willy. Lotty told me you were attacked a few days ago. Are you all right?"

"I'm doing better, thanks."

"I brought you some homemade chicken soup. Get your strength back. Be careful, it's hot."

Chapter 12

After two weeks recuperating, I peered at my image in the bathroom mirror and carefully lifted the bandage from my forehead. The injury healed well, but it looked as if an inch-long scar was forming. I delicately rubbed a finger along the spot; the skin was sensitive there.

I shaved, dressed, and then rode the tram with Lotty to rehearsal. There were no kisses from her at the entrance to the Concertgebouw; I shrugged it off, and went inside.

It was my first time playing with the orchestra since our last performance in the states. Mr. Sonata and the orchestra members gave me a wonderful welcome back; we had cake, coffee and tea beforehand.

I settled onto my chair next to Woodrow Herman, and the woodwind section tuned.

"You sound a bit sharp, Mr. Maze," the first chair clarinetist stated.

I adjusted my reed and tuned again.

"That's better," Mr. Herman said.

The conductor raised his baton, and we practiced the music for our upcoming holiday concert in Rome. I had some difficulty concentrating while we quickly ran through one composition after another. It seemed like I had to force the notes out of my instrument, sensing it had a problem. To make matters worse, I was having a migraine.

"Your intonation sounds a bit off, Mr. Maze," the first-chair clarinetist said during a coffee and bathroom break.

"It does."

Rehearsal ended, I swabbed my clarinet, took it apart and placed it in the case.

"Have you been practicing?" Mr. Herman inquired.

"I could do with more."

"Perhaps your clarinet needs a little tune up. I'd have a repairman look at it before our concert in Rome. That's three days from now."

"Yes. I know, Mr. Herman."

I briefly chatted with Lotty before leaving the Concertgebouw; she appeared to be more interested in conversing with her old friend, Eduardo, the tuba player who used to live in my flat.

I took a taxi to the music store, and the woodwind technician gave my clarinet a thorough inspection.

"I have some bad news for you, Mr. Maze," the instrument repairman announced. "I discovered a slight crack in your instrument. Was it dropped?"

"A few weeks ago," I replied.

"That's a shame. How'd that happen?"

"Someone tried to steal it from me. Can it be fixed?"

"Even if I could, it wouldn't sound good enough for a professional orchestra. I highly suggest you buy a new clarinet."

Chapter 13

The day before Christmas, I arrived in Rome with a brand-new instrument. After registering for a room at the Ritz Carlton, I washed up and strolled down to the hotel's bar, where some orchestra members, including Lotty and Eduardo, were having cocktails. I pulled up a stool beside them and ordered a whiskey.

"Hi, everyone."

"Hey, Willy. Ready for your debut concert back?" Lotty asked.

"Guess so. Hi, Eduardo. *Como esta?*"

"*Bien gracias.*"

"When's our sound check?" I asked.

"Two hours from now," Lotty replied.

After an early dinner at the hotel, I put on my tux and took the shuttle to the Auditorium Parco Della Musica in Rome. The orchestra had a sound check 45 minutes before the Christmas Eve show.

While I sucked on a new clarinet reed, Woodrow Herman greeted me backstage. "Good evening, Mr. Maze. I hope you're prepared for tonight's performance."

"Hello, Woodrow. Yes, I am."

"Good to see that your clarinet problem was sorted out. It looks nice."

"Thanks. It's a top-of-the-line Selmer."

"Bet that cost you a pretty penny."

"It did," I replied while gently rubbing the scar along my forehead.

That night in Rome, the concert hall was filled to capacity. Christmas ornaments glittered and glowed inside and outside the theater.

I took my seat, opened the music on my stand, and the clarinet section tuned. Afterward, a woman came out to introduce the orchestra and our 5' 1" Japanese conductor. He briskly appeared on stage to a boisterous applause, positioning himself at an elevated conductor's post; he tapped his wand, raised his arms, and we began our first composition of the evening: a medley of Christmas music by Handel, Bach, Mozart, and Verdi.

I laboriously got through those tunes. Tchaikovsky's Nutcracker Suite was next. It went well, up until the musician next to me, Geraldine, who was formerly Gerald, passed some ugly smelling gas, and someone in the audience had sneezed really loud; I played three embarrassingly wrong notes prior to Mr. Herman's clarinet solo, and he just about choked on his mouthpiece. The conductor gave me a what-the-fuck look. And the Christmas Eve performance ended with a lukewarm applause. The little conductor bowed sheepishly, and the curtain closed.

Backstage, a freckle-face bassoonist, the entire brass section, the first chair violinist, and Mr. Herman, all gave me looks.

Eduardo, the tuba player, asked me while Lotty and I were about to leave the concert hall: "*Que paso*, Willy?"

"I don't know, Eduardo. Guess, I had an off night."

"*Si. Muy malo.*"

As the tuba player slowly walked away, I noticed his eyes were glued on Lotty's backside.

She and I conversed while drinking brandy in a little café near the hotel.

"I can't believe how you played tonight, Willy—what happened to you?"

"I don't know. Think it was those new reeds I used. And I lost my concentration when that guy in the audience sneezed."

"That was a big screw-up."

"I know."

"Make sure it doesn't happen again—makes us all sound bad."

"What's going on with you and Eduardo?" I inquired.

"We're just old friends—he helps me out with stuff."

"What kind of stuff?"

"It's not important, Willy. I'm going back to my room. I'm exhausted."

Later that evening at the hotel while filling a bucket from an ice machine down the hall, I secretly observed the tuba player knock on Lotty's door. She opened it, and appeared in a sexy blue negligee; the provocatively attired woman quickly pulled the tuba player inside. And I knew then that Eduardo was doing more than just *helping her out with stuff.*

In the same concert hall in Rome, our Christmas day performance went without major incident.

The city of Florence was next on our tour schedule. The orchestra brought down the house with two performances in the Teatro Verdi.

It was at the Teatro Alla Scala in Milan, I thanked God we weren't performing in Sicily, or I might have been dead. The orchestra was playing a composition by Mozart, when I lost my train of thought and mistakenly played two bars in the wrong time signature. I threw the entire woodwind section completely off-tempo. And needless to say, we weren't encouraged to do an encore that evening. Mr. Sonata was so mad, he flipped me the bird after the curtain closed. Mr. Herman pitched a fit also. Lotty completely ignored me backstage, making out with Eduardo while sitting on his big lap. I slunk back to the hotel in a taxi by my myself.

The next morning at the hotel, before the roadies, sound-crew and orchestra members boarded four buses to Venice, I had a meeting with the Japanese conductor and Mr. Lewison. They noticed the difference in my playing. Mr. Sonata apologized for his rude gesture the night before while the orchestra manager directed his attention on me.

"The company has had much success with you, Mr. Maze. And I'm really sorry to be the one to tell you this, but we've decided to terminate your contract. We feel it would be best for everyone."

"Yeah, I understand."

"You'll be paid for the rest of the season," Mr. Lewison said. "Those are the terms in your contract."

We shook hands, and I sadly watched while they and some more orchestra members hurriedly boarded a bus in front of the hotel.

Totally devastated, I returned home to Amsterdam and fell into a depression. Lotty called me a couple days later to inform me she was getting engaged to Eduardo, and she never wanted to see, or hear from me again. I wasn't surprised. And I fell into an even deeper depression.

Chapter 14

January 1983

After playing my clarinet outside the freezing entrance to Central Station in Amsterdam, I put my instrument away, gathered the money I earned, and then quickly walked to Plato's. A seedy, yet amicable little pub on the same walking street I was attacked six months earlier; it was alive with an assortment of customers: Dutch locals, philosophers, drug dealers, the occasional tourist, expatriates, Irish, British, and American men and women.

When I entered Plato's, the juke box was playing *Every Breath You Take*, a song by the Police. I set my instrument case on the floor, sat on a barstool, and then a bunch of coins jangled in the pockets of my warm winter coat. I rubbed my hands together as the bartender, a Dutch woman, came over and asked me what I wanted to drink.

"Cognac please. Remy Martin."

"You just come from playing?" asked a blond-haired guy seated next to me. From his voice, he sounded like an American.

"Yeah. It's cold out there."

"Hi, I'm Johnstone."

"Willy."

"Is that a clarinet in there?" he asked.

"Yeah."

"I'm also a street musician. I play the banjo."

"What kind of music do you play?" I asked.

"Bluegrass, folk, and my own weird style of jazz. How 'bout you?"

"Mostly classical. Some Cole Porter and Benny Goodman tunes."

"No kidding. We should jam sometime. Cole Porter is one of my favorite composers," Johnstone stated.

"I'd be into that. So, what's this place all about?" I asked.

"A lot of street musicians in town hang out here. Sometimes we practice in the back room."

"Where you from, Johnstone?"

"Santa Barbara, California."

"You surf?"

"Never. Do a shot with me? I'm buying."

"What?"

"Jack Daniels."

"Why not."

"Mario?"

"Yah, Johnstone?"

"Two shots of Jack, please."

"Power!" the man loudly grunted, and prepared our drinks. The wild-eyed man placed the shots down, and Johnstone and I toasted.

After a couple of weeks hanging out and jamming with the banjo player in the back room at Plato's, he and I formed a duo, and we became fast friends. We started performing in pubs and private parties. Once the weather warmed up, we busked the side-walk cafes around town. Even though I no longer performed with the orchestra, I still had plenty of music in my blood.

On an unusually warm day in March, Johnstone and I performed at the cafes near the red-light district. Afterward, we returned to Plato's and headed for the back room to count the cash we made from the gig.

"How'd we do?" I asked.

"Seventy-five Guilders and two five-dollar notes a piece."

"Not bad."

"I may have some good paying work for us in the near future, Willy."

"Playing in a club?"

"It's not a music gig. The money's a lot better than that."

"What kind of work is it?" I asked.

"Involves a bit of traveling and delivering a specific type of merchandise."

"I've never been a good salesman, Johnstone. Aside for selling sandwiches and knishes in my father's deli."

"You wouldn't be selling anything, Willy. Only delivering it."

"If it's smuggling drugs—you can count me out," I said.

"Absolutely not."

"What is it then?"

"Transporting diamonds and other precious gems."

"Are you serious?"

"We'd make a lot more money than what we're currently earning."

"How much are you talking about?"

"That depends on the quality and the quantity of gems we deliver. Think about it, Willy. It involves smuggling contraband, so I wouldn't mention this to anyone. Especially in this place. Undercover cops come in here sometimes."

"Of course not. Let's grab a beer."

Before I went to sleep that night, I mulled-over Johnstone's proposal. *I definitely could use the extra money for paying bills on my apartment. And the savings I accrued from the orchestra work wasn't going to last forever.* I gave him an answer in the morning.

Chapter 15

On the first day of Spring, I rode the train from Central Station to Brussels, Belgium. It was my first smuggling assignment, and I was slightly on edge, scheduled to pick up and deliver four kilos of cut and polished diamonds to Munich, Germany. Johnstone told me the day before, the contraband would be inside a small suitcase in a locker at the train station in Brussels. I was to meet him there.

I got off the train in Belgium, and went inside the old brick station. I purchased a one-way ticket to Munich, and noticed Johnstone standing nearby. His long, straight blond hair was oiled back, and he had a Styrofoam coffee cup in one hand. And a blue, well-used suitcase on the floor beside him.

"Morning, Johnstone."

"Hi, Willy. Got you a coffee, no cream no sugar."

"Thanks. The goods in there?" I asked while pointing to the tired-looking suitcase.

"Yep. Are you ready for this?"

"I guess."

"Relax. Take some deep breaths," he advised. "Hope you brought your passport."

"It's in my pocket."

"What time's your train?" Johnstone inquired.

"Eleven fifteen."

"We better make a move. Here, take the coffee. You'll be all right. Just relax, Willy."

Whenever someone tells me to relax, I usually do the opposite. I held the suitcase handle so tight it burned the palm of my hand. It had no wheels. I picked it up, judging it weighed no more than seven pounds. While we walked through the station lobby, one of the latches on the suitcase sprung open. I heard my friend's voice in my head: *Just relax, Willy.*

"Oh, crap—the suitcase is weirding out on me, dude. Where'd ya get this?"

"Keep walking. We'll fix it in a moment. Just relax."

"Could you stop saying that."

"Sorry."

Just then, a station policeman approached us from the opposite direction. I lowered my head and innocently looked at the floor, praying the other latch wouldn't pop open. Nothing happened. We went over to a bench, and I secured the luggage. Johnstone and I left the building and stood on the chilly train platform. I deeply sighed while loosening my grip on the suitcase handle. My train was late as it idled close by. I forced a smile, shook

Johnstone's large hand while a high-pitched whistle sounded. It was time to go. He handed me a slip of paper with a phone number on it.

"Call me when you get to the station in Munich," he said. "And don't let the suitcase out of your site—or we'll be owing the boss big time."

I put the phone number in my wallet while a conductor announced in a discordant groan: "All aboard for Germany."

I balanced the coffee, stepped onto the train and into a vacant car with blue leather seats. It wasn't a particularly modern train, but clean. I put the coffee cup in a holder, daypack next to me, and then carefully lifted the small suitcase onto a rack above the seat. I neurotically glanced up at it a couple times, settled in, and then placed my ticket and passport on the empty seat beside me. I was the only passenger inside the car.

I waited.

The train doors closed.

Too late to turn back now, I said to myself.

The train jerked forward, and started rolling.

Johnstone had mentioned once it crossed the border into Germany, the first stop would be Aachen; a small town where someone might check my passport, or open the suitcase, but it wasn't very likely this time of day. So, he said.

I started thinking: *How the hell did I get into this crazy business? I should be playing my clarinet on a street corner somewhere. And why haven't I seen the conductor yet? I don't know if I'm being paid enough to do this kind of work. I should have brought something to read. Just relax. You'll be all right.*

The train stopped in Antwerp, Belgium, and Lotty Lipshitz crisscrossed my mind. *Tough luck, I guess. That's the way the gluten-free cookie crumbles. I certainly didn't miss the woman's blabber mouth parrot and masturbating love bird.* I still hadn't told my parents we broke up, or about losing my job with the orchestra.

At a small town after Antwerp, a skinny man dressed in black, a young priest, boarded the car I was in. He carried a book in one hand, and a small bag in the other. He noticed my blue suitcase above the vacant seat opposite me.

He asked in English, "Is there someone sitting there?"

"No."

He sat, opened his book, and turned the pages while I closed my eyes and slept. When I awoke, the priest was standing in the aisle and tapping my shoulder. I heard the announcement for the station. Aachen. My heart skipped a beat.

"My apologies sir, but I saw that you were asleep, and I thought this might be your stop," the clergyman said.

"It's not, I'm going to Munich."

"I'm sorry for disturbing you. Have a blessed day, brother."

"You as well, Father."

The train wheels slowly moved again.

From the corner of my eye, I saw a conductor draw near; he asked me in a formal German accent: "Ticket and passport please."

My pulse increased.

"Is there something wrong?" he asked.

"No. Why?"

"You look a little nervous."

"Do I?"

I handed the conductor the requested items, and he silently gawked behind a pair of gold, wire-rimmed glasses. He stamped my ticket, gave it back, and then curiously opened my passport with a meticulous air of authority.

"American?"

"Yes."

"Where did you get on the train?"

"Brussels. I started in Amsterdam."

"Smoking the wacky weed there?" he asked with a half-chuckle.

"I don't like marijuana, sir. Can't stand the smell of it."

"But you have other nice drugs in your luggage you plan to sell in Germany? Perhaps some ecstasy, or LSD? Drugs are verboten in our country you know."

"I would never do such a thing."

"*Nein?* Then what is your main purpose for visiting Germany?" he interrogated, suddenly looking a bit like Adolf Eichman. (The nazi officer from World War Two.)

"I'm on vacation."

"Ah, *das ist gut.* It's your luggage up there?"

"Yes, sir."

"Is it locked?"

"No," I replied, swallowing hard. "Should I take it down for you?"

"I can open it from there."

At that moment, I felt myself shrink into a tiny person while the seat increased in size. My armpits freely dripped perspiration as the conductor opened the suitcase, rustled through it a few moments and then closed it. He stamped my passport and politely handed it back to me.

"Enjoy your vacation, Mr. Maze. And don't lose your marbles while you're in Germany."

"*Danke Schoen.*"

"*Bitte schoen.*"

The conductor turned away and laughed as he left the car. I wondered why he would say such a thing, but it didn't matter, because I was over the biggest hurdle, no more borders to cross. He must have missed the diamonds for some strange reason. The train rode on. And a heavy weight was lifted off my shoulders.

An hour and a half later, I viewed the rolling white hills of Bavaria. The train coasted into Munich station. I got off, found a pay phone, and then dialed the number Johnstone had given me. A man with a German accent answered the phone.

"Yah, who is this?"

"Willy. Can I speak to Johnstone please."

"Just a moment."

"Hello."

"I'm in Munich, Johnstone."

"Great. Take the number 10 bus at the train station and get off at the Marienplatz stop, then go to the big square and wait for me by the gold statue of the Virgin Mary."

I exchanged some money, exited the station, and then looked for the bus stand. I got on the #10, paid the driver, and asked him how many stops to the Marienplatz square. Four, he replied. I found a seat in the front next to a guy who looked like a college student; books were stacked on his lap, and he kept looking at my suitcase with a shit-eating-grin. It made me paranoid. The bus door closed, and the driver took off.

At the Marienplatz square, I watched the late afternoon sun reflect off the gold-colored statue. I handed a homeless man a dollar and went around to the other side, where Johnstone appeared.

"Hey, Willy."

"We got a stop meeting like this man," I said.

"Let's go—I parked the car around the corner."

"Didn't know you had a car."

"I rented it in Brussels."

We left the square, headed to a side street nearby, and then I followed Johnstone to a white, four-door Mercedes. I placed the suitcase in the trunk, and we drove to a more residential neighborhood of Munich. Johnstone parked, I removed the suitcase, and we went inside a 12-story apartment building. We got off the elevator on the second floor, down a hallway, and knocked on a door. A bald-headed man opened it.

"He's a little late, Johnstone," the man said. "The boss doesn't like that."

"Willy's train had a delay."

"C'mon in. Hi, I'm Curly Joe."

"Nice to me you," I said.

"Anybody want a drink?" Mr. Joe asked.

"Red wine," Johnstone replied.

"A whiskey on the rocks, please."

Mr. Joe fixed our drinks, then he sat on an armchair with a bottle of dark beer.

"Let's check out the diamonds. Open the luggage, Willy Maze."

I released the latches on the suitcase and excitedly opened Pandora's box. I took out four large, clear plastic bags filled with a colorful assortment of marbles.

Johnstone and Mr. Joe laughed.

"I know these aren't diamonds," I stated.

"No, they aren't Willy," Mr. Joe said. "It was only a test. To see if you could do it. You still get paid. Here's your money. A thousand dollars. Count it."

"Thanks."

Surprised, yet relieved, I gulped down the Canadian whiskey and counted the cash. All in one-hundred-dollar bills. I smiled, placed the money into my pants pocket, and then took a marble out and rolled it between my fingers. I realized then, why the German conductor had said what he said on the train. I felt like an idiot, but at least I was a thousand dollars richer.

"Now that you've passed our little test, Mr. Maze, your next trip will be with the real jewels. Yah?"

"Sure."

"*Das ist wunderbar*. Let's celebrate."

Mr. Joe stroked his shiny bald head, picked up his beer and had a swig.

I stayed in a Munich hotel for the night, and returned to Amsterdam the next day.

In the seven months that followed, with Johnstone as the intermediary, I successfully delivered over a half a million dollars' worth of diamonds, cultured pearls, precious gems, silver and gold, by train, car, or ship, to Munich, Rome, London, Paris, Stockholm, Copenhagen, Zurich, and Belfast.

Chapter 16

On a prickly hot July morning in 1983, I cranked the air conditioner in my apartment in Amsterdam, then put two slices of raisin bread in the toaster when the telephone rang in the living room.

"Hey, Willy, it's Johnstone."

"You back from California?"

"Got in last night. The boss called me. Said we'll have some more work soon."

"To Munich?"

"No, it involves a lot more traveling than that. I'll be at your apartment in thirty minutes."

"Cool."

The smoke detector went off in the kitchen. *Damn—I burned the toast!* I opened all the windows and shut off the alarm. I sliced a banana and ate a bowl of granola instead. Twenty minutes later, Johnstone arrived.

"Hey, Willy. Good to see you. You burn something?"

"Some toast earlier."

"You've been doing a phenomenal job, Willy. The boss told me to tell you. You got a bonus."

"Great."

My friend handed me a sealed envelope.

"I appreciate that. Tell the boss I said thank you."

"I will. Why don't you make a fresh pot of coffee. I'll fill you in about our next gig. It's pretty involved."

Chapter 17

A week after Johnstone informed me about our next assignment, I entered the lobby of the Amsterdam Hotel; the place John Lennon and Yoko Ono once celebrated their honeymoon and bed-in for peace on March 20, 1969. I sadly flashed back to the Amsterdam Philharmonic while listening to a live trio play classical music on the piano, cello and violin, from a corner of the lobby. It got dark out.

I went up to my room, sat on the bed, and then looked out a window overlooking a Dam Square bustling with tourists. Lights illuminated the Royal Palace across from the piazza while some English guys jammed in a blues band.

I heard a knock on the door.

"Who is it?"

"Johnstone."

I let him in.

"Good evening, Willy."

"Everything all set with the merchandise, Johnstone?"

"Yeah, it's packed in two locked suitcases in the trunk of the blue Saab 9000 and ready to go. There's about two million worth of gems, so be sure the car is locked at all times."

"Two million's a shit load of marbles, man."

"That's for sure," Johnstone said as I was handed the keys. "The car's in the parking garage in the back of the hotel. Second level, spot 27. Write it down. It's a long haul to Greece, and then the ship to Haifa. Here's your directions, boarding pass and boat ticket. Set your alarm for five, and go. Good luck and safe travels."

"Thanks."

"Call me when ya get to Austria," Johnstone said as he opened the door to leave.

Chapter 18

Damn it! I overslept. I jumped out of bed, dressed, and then hurriedly filled a to-go-cup in the lobby of the Amsterdam Hotel.

In the parking garage, I took the elevator to level 2, found space 27, and then unlocked a cobalt blue Saab 9000 stick shift. I drove it once before, making a run to Sweden carrying $100,000 in rubies, silver necklaces, diamonds and pearls. I tossed my suitcase and daypack in the trunk before sitting behind the wheel and revving the 16-valve engine.

Exiting the garage, I passed some twinkling lights on a canal, drove through Amsterdam, and then listened to the BBC from London. I sipped the coffee, bit into a rice cake, and then cracked the windows some, feeling the brisk morning air on my unshaven face. The sun eventually appeared in the rearview mirror.

Boy, when I reminisce about it now, that car could really fly. Time did also.

After breakfast at a diner in Nijmegen, Holland, I approached the border into Kranenburg, Germany. The guard came out, wearing those funny looking trousers called *lederhosen*. (The knickers with the suspenders.) I laughed as he nosed around the front and back of the car.

I rolled down my window, and the guard curtly asked: "Passport, *bitte!*"

"Here you go. Sorry."

He examined my identification. "What's so funny, Villy Maze?"

"I just remembered a joke a friend told me once," I replied while diverting my eyes from his silly looking trousers.

"Tell me the joke."

"It's not that funny—you really wanna hear it?"

"Yes—tell me the joke. *Schnell!*"

"Okay. If you're an American in the living room, then what are you in the bathroom?"

The border guard scratched his head and thought: "I don't know. Vhat?"

"Eur-a-pean. Get it? You're a pee'n."

He laughed while tugging on his blue suspenders.

"I love it—that's quite amusing. Why are you visiting Germany?"

"I'm vacationing in Europe. I'll be traveling to many countries."

"I love American humor," the border guard stated. "My wife, Gretchen and I, watch Seinfeld almost every night."

"Who's your favorite character?" I asked.

"Jerry, of course. Yours?"

"It's a toss-up between George and Elaine," I replied.

"Ah. What do you do for a living?"

"I'm a professional musician."

"What instrument do you play?"

"Clarinet."

He x-rayed the car, stamped my passport, and then gave it back to me.

"Have a lovely vacation young man."

"*Danke.*"

The border guard waved me through; I released the clutch, got on the autobahn, and then put the pedal to the metal.

Miles later, I entered Austria through an unattended border crossing. Shortly after, I encountered a hitchhiker; a bearded man wearing a grey three-piece suit, silver watch chain slung in front, a briefcase, and an unlit cigar in his hand.

Suppose I could give him a ride.

He appeared to be examining his own thoughts. *I really could use the company.* I drove onto the shoulder and stopped.

"Catch a ride with you, sir?" the hitchhiker asked with a distinct European accent.

"How far ya going?"

"Vienna," he replied.

"Hop in."

The man climbed into the back seat, looked at his pocket watch and declared: "I hope I won't be late for my two o'clock appointment."

"Are you going to a doctor's appointment?"

"I am the doctor. My name is Dr. Sigmund Freud."

"The famous psychoanalyst?" I asked while the road made a slight dip in reality.

"The one and only."

"It's an honor to meet you, Dr. Freud."

"Likewise. And you are?"

"Willy Maze."

"Interesting last name. According to my quick analysis of you. Your name suggests you are somewhat of a labyrinth. A maze. Willy the maze. Like all of us, you are seeking a specific destination, and must follow paths to lead you there. Tell me if I'm incorrect."

"That's a pretty accurate interpretation, doctor."

"Excellent. And what is that gadget?"

"A car phone."

"A telephone?"

"Exactly. Just a more modern version."

"Can I call my office with it?"

"Of course."

"I wouldn't have the slightest idea of how to use this car phone."

"I can call on the hands free."

"Hans free? What is that?"

"I'll show you. What's your office number?"

"I don't know it. I never call my office."

"Don't you have a business card on you?"

"Good idea," the man said as he removed a white card from his wallet.

I pulled onto the shoulder, and the good doctor read the phone number for me.

"Four-eight-four-nine-zero-seven-five-five-nine-nine."

I placed the call, and it rang three times before a woman answered in German.

"Talk to the person, doctor."

"Yes, hello Mrs. Frieberg. This is Dr. Freud speaking. I'm calling to inform you, I may be a little late for Carl Jung's two o'clock appointment."

"I'm sorry, Dr. Freud, but you must have the wrong number. This is the Irving Berlin Piano Repair shop in Vienna. Goodbye."

"What are you going to do now?" I asked while veering back onto the highway.

"I haven't a clue. Change my profession perhaps. Speaking of professions—what is it that you do for a living, Mr. Macy?"

"Maze. I deliver diamonds."

"Well, that's an interesting occupation. Have you always done this type of work?"

"No, I used to play the clarinet in an orchestra."

"Your job involves a bit of traveling, I surmise?"

"It does. I'm currently on my way to Greece."

"Sounds more fun than my work. All I do is listen to patients moan about their mental state all day. It's not a bad living mind you. And I can't complain. I've become quite famous at it."

"I think your exit is coming up in two kilometers, doctor. You want me to drop you off in downtown Vienna?"

"Just let me off on the side of the road—like you found me."

"Well, I hope you're on time for your appointment."

"What appointment would that be?"

"Never mind."

I stopped the car, let the supposed therapist out, and then glanced in my side-view mirror. He had his hand on his hip, the half-smoked cigar in the other hand, and a deeply contemplative expression.

I smiled, turned on the radio, and then listened to a jazz station for the next 100 kilometers or so.

I read once that the side-effects of driving long hours may cause hallucinations. I suppose that's what happened to me on that lengthy journey through Europe. It would be utter *nonsense* to think I picked up Dr. Sigmund Freud hitchhiking. *He probably came from a mental institution down the road.*

At a rest area, I stopped and called Johnstone.

"I'm in Austria. Two hours from Vienna."

"How's it going?"

"I'm good. But exhausted. Gonna find a hotel room soon."

"Call me when you get to Yugoslavia."

"Will do."

A short distance more, I drove into a small village called Freudenberg, ironically enough. I climbed a steep hill, where a rustic looking lodging sat. It was called The Dragonfly Inn. I parked in front and noticed a man and his daughter standing by a white van. A brown Doberman playfully jumped out of the vehicle and ran toward me. I pet the animal, and it happily urinated on a bush.

"He's a bit too friendly at times," the dog's owner stated while his young daughter restrained him.

"Sorry sir. Not everyone likes dogs. Behave Roget," the girl said.

"I do—is that his name—Roget?" I asked.

"Yes, it is," the father replied. "I named him after my thesaurus. I'm a writer."

"Good boy. He's the most congenial Doberman I've ever met. I'm Willy by the way."

"Nice to meet you. I'm Vermont Forever. That's my daughter, Strawberry Fields."

"We better get ready for dinner sweetie."

"Yes, Dad. Come on, Roget."

"Are you from Vermont?" I asked the man.

"No. I grew up in Gainesville, Florida."

"I'm from the states also. How do you like the hotel?"

"It's fine. The owners are a little strange though," Mr. Forever answered while the smell of homecooked food wafted through a window. The short-haired hound lifted his head and detected the garlicky odor as well.

Chapter 19

Windchimes sounded when I pulled open the door to the inn; I set my suitcase on the floor by the front desk and tapped a chrome bell twice.

"Heard you the first time," a bearded man announced from a rocking chair. "Welcome to the Dragonfly Inn."

"Thanks."

I couldn't believe it when I saw him; it was the man I had given a ride to only a couple of hours before. He was dressed in the same three-piece suit, unlit cigar in one hand, a pocket watch in the other, and a thought-provoking look on his face.

"Good evening, Dr. Freud. I'm really surprised to see you here."

"You must be mistaking me for someone else. My name is Jack Kirkland. I'm one of the owners of this fine establishment."

"It wasn't you I picked up hitchhiking on the Autobahn a couple hours ago?"

"I should hope not," the man replied. "Everybody who comes here thinks I'm Freud. I'm a big tourist attraction in Freudenberg. I should sell tickets to people who want to make conversation with the infamous doctor. I'd get rich quick."

"Sorry about that, but you do have a striking resemblance to the man."

"You can check in with my wife—she's at the front desk now. And by the way, I'm a retired pastor. And if it's any interest to you—my cat's name is Bentley."

The large male, amber-furred tabby meowed and looked away from me bored.

"Rita, will you help this young gentleman. He's in need of a room."

"Yes, Jack," a friendly old woman said, speaking English with a Dutch accent, "Good evening, sir. Will it be just you checking in?"

"Yes, ma'am. I'm only staying one night."

"I have a lovely suite with a splendid view of the Austrian Alps. It's $150.00 a night. That includes a full dinner with dessert, a glass of wine, and a continental breakfast. We take Visa, Mastercard, and cash is king of course. I'm sorry, I didn't get your name."

"Mr. Maze," I said while counting some American money and stacking it on the counter.

The woman counted the money again, placed it in her cleavage, and then wrote me out a receipt.

"What time is dinner served?"

"Right now, Mr. Maze. From 6 o'clock to 8 o'clock. Breakfast is from 7:00 to 9:30. Here's your key. Room 27, on the second floor. The elevator is right over there."

"Thank you."

I took my little suitcase, approached the elevator, and then exchanged glances with a sharp-eyed woman with scaly looking skin, and black hair raised in a windblown bob. She wore a pink, snug-fitting jogging suit, and winced, probably because of my strong body odor. We passed, and I went up to my room and washed up for dinner. I put on a new shirt, a sports jacket, and some underarm deodorant.

At the dining room entrance, Bentley the cat, rubbed against my leg and purred, acting as if he was the maître d. I followed the animal through the room, and he seated me at a table along a wall, where a framed print of Leonardi da Vince's Mona Lisa hung. The cat pranced away and was replaced by a waiter who set a basket of rolls on the table, filled a water glass, and then handed me a menu with a limited selection of entrees.

The young woman, who I passed at the elevator earlier, was seated at a table nearby. A glass of red wine and a bottle accompanied her. She sported a stately air, a black leather skirt, a white, low-cut blouse that revealed a scaly chest, diamond necklace, and a ruby-colored lipstick that embellished her well-proportioned figure. I returned my focus on the menu.

"I highly recommend the cream of mushroom soup, Mr. Maze," announced a waiter with a thin brown bewhiskered growth under his little pink nose. "The Kirkland's grow their own mushrooms and most other vegetables from their farm next door."

"They must be fresh then," I stated.

"They certainly are."

That's weird, I thought. *I hadn't noticed a farm when I drove up the hill.*

"I'll have the soup. Is the salmon fresh or farm-raised?"

"Fresh from the Danube," the waiter replied, brushing his shoulder like a flea had landed there.

"The baked fish then. With the fried potatoes, green salad, and a glass of Sauvignon Blanc. Please."

I unfolded a cloth napkin, and shortly after, the waiter returned with a piping hot bowl of soup. While stirring the grayish white pottage, I raised my head and noticed the young woman nearby was exposing her cleavage and flirting with me. I smiled and waved.

She enticingly asked me in a French accent: "Would you like to enjoy me for dessert later?"

That would be some dessert, I thought. I lifted my ruddy colored eyebrows and assumed English wasn't her first language.

"I'd be delighted to. After I eat my entrée. And I don't mean to be rude, but the correct way of saying that is, *would you like to join me for dessert.*"

"*Oui.* How stupid of me," she stated, and laughed.

The server removed my soup bowl, and he replaced it with the baked fish. It freaked me out a little, because it came whole, head still attached, its black eyes pensively fixed on me. I curiously jabbed the quivering salmon with my fork, eating the salad and potato instead.

I informed the waiter I'd be moving to the table nearby, taking my wine glass and sitting in the chair opposite the woman. I shook her hand and introduced myself:

"Hi, I'm Willy."

"Say hey, Billy. I'm Merlot Jenkins."

"That's a very uncommon name," I said.

She laughed and turned the front of the wine bottle to face me.

"I'm drinking Merlot, Billy—I was only kidding. *Relax*."

I read the label, "Jenkin's Merlot. California 1976." I lifted my wine glass. "To your health."

"Cheers. My real name is Marie Antoinette."

"Serious?"

"Why wouldn't I be. You want a glass of red wine?"

"I'll stick with my white, thanks," I replied as the waiter came by to ask us about dessert.

"I'll have the strawberry shortcake," the comical, yet eccentric young lady answered. "Extra whipped cream, Bentley."

"Yes, ma'am. For you, sir?"

"The Black Forest cake. And a cognac. Remy Martin."

The waiter left.

"Isn't Bentley the cat's name?"

"I haven't seen a cat around here," the scaly skinned woman replied. "Where you from, Billy?"

"New York originally. And yourself?"

"Born and raised in Paris. Excuse me, I have to use the little girl's room."

"Sure."

When Ms. Antoinette left the table, her perfume left behind an alluring, although fishy sort of air.

The waiter brought my cognac and our desserts, and I scarfed half my cake before the Parisian woman returned. When she did, I saw that she had put on a strawberry-blond wig, and a head band adorned with costume diamonds and colorful bird feathers. Her face was powdered with an alabaster white make-up, and it looked as if she had changed into a different blouse. Clothing from a much earlier era.

"Sorry I took so long, Billy. See you like chocolate."

"One of my weaknesses. Love your wig."

"What the fuck are you talking about, Billy? —it's my real hair."

"Oh, I'm sorry."

The French woman scowled and forked a healthy bite of strawberry short cake, leaving a shmear of whipped cream on her upper lip; she grinned, stuck out her tongue, and then erotically licked it off.

"I love strawberry shortcake, Billy."

"I see."

"Do you know what Marie Antoinette used to say when she was the Queen of France?"

"What?"

"Let them eat cake!" the woman shouted. "So, what are you doing in Austria?"

"Delivering jewelry."

"Really?"

"Yeah."

"Have any samples on you?"

"I wish. What's your occupation?"

"I'm a pilot for Lufthansa. I have a few days off, so, I thought I'd do some hiking in the alps. I usually come here when I fly into Vienna."

"How long have you been a pilot?"

"About fifteen years. Wanna know a little secret, Billy?"

"What's that?"

"The inn's owner, Mr. Kirkland, grows his own mushrooms."

"I know—the waiter told me."

"I mean the kind that make you hallucinate."

"How do you know that?" I inquired.

"Mr. Kirkland told me."

"Wish I would've known that before I had the soup."

"It's fine."

"You ever try any of his mushrooms?—the magic ones."

"Once," Marie replied. "I'll never do that again."

"Why?"

"I ended up climbing to the top of the Matterhorn. Naked."

"Bet that caused quite a stir with the other hikers."

"Nobody saw me, Billy. It was at night."

"Oh."

Our conversation was beginning to weird me out; the longer I conversed with the woman who called herself Marie Antoinette, the more she appeared like the person I'd seen on oil paintings of the Queen of France, in a museum in Amsterdam.

"I'm bored and hot. Wanna go skinny dipping with me?"

"Where? They don't have a pool here," I said as her bare toes massaged my inner thigh. It titillated me some. I felt that blushing bulge again while she brushed against my erection and laughed.

"We can go in the pond out back. It's nice in the summertime. Refreshing on these humid nights."

"Have you been in it before?" I asked.

"A couple times last year. It's clean."

"What about water moccasins, or snapping turtles?"

"There are none. Only frogs and fish."

"Maybe we should digest our food awhile," I suggested while catching a hint of the woman's perfume again.

"You're right. I'll order a coffee. Bentley?"

"Yes, Ms. Antoinette?"

"An espresso please."

"One for you, sir?"

"No, thanks," I answered while noticing how much the waiter's face resembled the cat. *Bizarre.*

After Marie drank her coffee, and I finished my cognac, we left the dining room, got into the elevator, and then French-kissed on the way up to the second floor. When the door opened, we were interrupted by the guy named Vermont. His dog started humping me, and he pulled him away. We laughed while exiting the elevator.

By coincidence, Marie's room was next to mine. I changed into a bathing suit, grabbed a bath towel, and then came out. She was already standing outside her door, dressed in a long pink skirt and ornate top with ribbons and ruffled blue sleeves. Quite flamboyant for a skinny dip, I would say. She had applied a fresh layer of scarlet lipstick that shimmered in the pheromone light.

"You ready?" I asked.

She whispered: "Say hey, Billy."

She rubbed her layered dress against me, licked my ear lobe with the tip of her tongue, and I felt the squamous skin on her face touch my cheek.

I thought to myself: *Maybe I'll get lucky tonight.*

"C'mon—we can take the back stairway—nobody will see us go through the lobby like this," the awkwardly dressed woman stated.

"After you, Marie."

We slowly walked to the end of the corridor, down a flight of stairs, and then left the air-conditioned building through a back exit.

The humidity outside was as thick as blood pudding. Something I never ate, and had no intention of eating in the future. I trailed the heavily dressed woman along a walkway leading to some concrete steps with wrought-iron handrails.

Bull frogs yodeled and crickets sang while a thick white mist hovered above the pond.

Marie unlocked her skirt, unbuttoned her top, unfastened a girdle, garter belts, stockings, bra and panties; she left it all in a pile by her feet—that didn't look like feet at all.

I took off my t-shirt, and she laughingly pulled my bathing suit down to my ankles. Her nude physique was barely visible through the mist.

"We're too loud. Someone might hear us, Marie."

"Who? The frogs."

She laughed while her spiny nipples pressed against my chest. We kissed before submerging ourselves into the icy alpine water. I came up for air, and the scaly skinned woman hugged her arms and legs around me. Her pubic bush tickled me while I looked up at the stars. I felt a silence as the woman released her slippery embrace and swam to the other side of the pond.

I felt something nibble on my penis. I reached into the water and batted away a foot-long fish. I stepped out of the pond and heard a twig snap nearby. Through the fog, I saw the silhouette of someone smoking a cigar and sitting on a bench.

His voice startled me: "Hello, Mr. Maze. Gorgeous evening, isn't it."

"Shit—who's that?"

"Jack Kirkland."

"Have you been sitting here all this time?" I asked while hunting for my towel, tee-shirt and bathing suit.

"Yes, I saw every dirty detail from this bench. You're a naughty man, Mr. Maze. Shame on you. You couldn't use your room?"

"I didn't realize you were here, Mr. Kirkland."

"I must admit, Mr. Maze. If I was your age and not married, I might have been tempted to do the same. I believe it's past my bedtime. Goodnight."

"Mine too," I said while I toweled my hair, gathered my things and was about to leave, when something large splashed from the water and wiggled on the ground.

"How was your swim, Billy?"

"Marie?"

"In the flesh."

I was horrified when I saw what was lying there: It wasn't a naked woman, but a large fish, wearing a diamond necklace and lips smeared a red tint, like the French woman had worn. A bottle and two glasses were placed beside the 120-pound carp.

"Have a seat, Billy," the strangely attired pond creature said as it sucked in air from its gills. "Join me for a nightcap?"

Chapter 20

Come sunrise at the inn, despite an unpleasant hangover, I enjoyed a splendid view of the Austrian Alps from my window. A note had been slipped under the door; I assumed it was from the woman I had dessert with last night. Marie Antoinette. I placed it in my shirt pocket, and went downstairs for breakfast.

A gray suited Mr. Kirkland, was in the lobby, rocking in his chair, holding his pocket watch, and petting his cat, Bentley.

"Top of the morning to you, Mr. Maze. Are you checking out today?"

"I am. Good morning, Jack."

"Well, I hope you've enjoyed your stay with us."

"I have, thanks. And do you mind if we kept what happened last night our little secret?"

"Why—what happened last night? I was fast asleep after dinner. Do tell me."

"Never mind. It's not that important. Is that French woman having breakfast?"

"I don't know of any French women staying at the hotel, Mr. Maze."

"She was here last night. Her first name is Marie. She works for Lufthansa. She told me she was a pilot."

"I'm sorry, but there's been no Marie, or pilots staying with us either, Mr. Maze."

"No worries."

I proceeded to the dining room, poured myself a cup of coffee, plated some cheese-filled strudel Mrs. Kirkland had baked, and then sat at the same table I was at last night.

I had another coffee while waiting for the French woman to turn up. She never did. The sun reflected off my gold wristwatch. It was eight o'clock. Before leaving the dining room, I read the note that was in my pocket:

Sitting with Shame

> Shame feels like a hole in which fear and sadness sit together. Huddled in the dark, around the searing flames of judgement. Judgement feeds her own fires, rising smoke obliterating the diamond-night-sky of self-worth. Sitting with fear and sadness, seek not to drive them from the fire's edge, but rather, hold their shaking hands. Be still and wait while the flames of judgement become the quietly glowing embers of

compassion. Invite then, a clearer upward gaze, and find a bit of the shimmering diamond self.

I placed the unsigned prose in my shirt pocket, got up from the table, and then rolled my little suitcase to the front desk. I thanked Mrs. Kirkland before leaving the hotel.

Chapter 21

As I apprehensively approached a deserted and bombed out border station, I left Austria, and entered what was then, the former Yugoslavia. Kranj was the first town I came to; it was desolate and looked as if a battle had taken place there recently. The streets were filled with decomposing bodies. Large vultures sat beside them; each one eyed me while I drove past.

After filling the gas tank in a war-torn Sarajevo, I was about to get back on the road when a group of soldiers surrounded the car.

"Identity papers!" ordered a soldier who was apparently in charge. Fortunately, he spoke some English. They sounded Russian. I gave the commanding officer my passport; he stroked his mean, Joseph Stalin mustache, and then turned the pages.

"American?" he asked.

"Yes. Are you Russian?"

"Shut up! What are you doing here?"

"I'm on my way to Greece. I don't want any trouble, Capitan."

"You are finished driving," the man said as he gave me the passport. "Give me all your money. Your watch too. You have any more jewelry?"

"No. Are you gonna let me go now?" I asked while my hands nervously grasped the steering wheel.

He laughed. The other soldiers joined in. He said something in Russian, and they readied their rifles.

"We're going to kill you now, American capitalist pig," the commanding soldier said while admiring my gold watch and haughtily placing a hand upon the car. He gave me an evil smile and spit.

"Could I make a phone call before you kill me?"

"To your lawyer?" he questioned and laughed. The other soldiers joined in.

"No, to a friend."

"Quickly!"

I dialed Johnstone's number in Amsterdam.

"Hey, Johnstone. It's Willy."

"Where are you? —I was expecting a call from you hours ago."

"I'm in Sarajevo. Having a slight problem. And the reception isn't too good here."

"Did you say the car broke down?"

"The car's fine. I've been detained by some unfriendly soldiers. I won't be seeing you in Tel Aviv."

"Why the hell not?"

"They're gonna shoot me. And probably take the car."

"What!" the middleman exclaimed.

"Finish phone call!" the Capitan shouted while the other soldiers impatiently held their rifles. "Out of the car. Stand over there."

I got out and the Capitan ordered the soldiers to aim their rifles at me.

Just then, a glaring red light shined through a cloud low in the sky. While the Capitan and the other soldiers gazed up at it (their weapons still aimed), the light flashed once, and the military men were scorched to ashes and their guns to metal dust.

I got in the car, called Johnstone back, and told him I was able to get myself out of the jam.

A few miles down the road, I passed Montenegro, and approached the towering mountains of northern Greece. On the craggy roadside, a backpacking hitchhiker dreamily appeared: A strong and youthful man dressed in white work clothes, a multi-colored skull cap, white gloves, white boots, and a pair of super dark sunglasses. He also possessed a black toolbox. His hair and beard were white as snow, and so long, I couldn't see where it ended. I downshifted, stopped on the shoulder, and the man walked up to my window and gave me the peace sign.

"Thanks for stopping, Willy."

"How far you going?"

"Mercury," the long-haired hitchhiker replied.

"Is that a town in Greece?"

"No, it's the closest planet to the sun. I have to do a little work there today—a temperature gauge is broken."

"Here, let me put your toolbox and backpack in the trunk." I got out, opened the rear access, and then attempted to lift the toolbox. "What's in here?— weighs a ton."

"Every tool in the universe, Mr. Maze. I better do that," he said while effortlessly lifting it.

"Hey, wait a minute. How do you know my name?"

"It's on your driver's license. I picked up your wallet back where those soldiers were about to kill you. And I have your watch also. I figured you might need it," he said handing me the items.

"That was nice of you—thanks. You saw what happened back at the gas station?"

"I saw it all."

"Judging by your toolbox, I assume you're some kind of repairman?"

"I like to think of myself as a 'jack of all trades' Mr. Maze. Do you mind if I drive? I always wanted to drive a stick. And I know the road a lot better than you do."

"Sure."

"Oh, there's something you need to do before we take off," the man said while he pulled some clothes out of his backpack.

"What's that?"

"The temperature is over 800 degrees on Mercury today. Put these on over your clothes. It'll protect you from the extreme heat."

The hitchhiker handed me a pair of white gloves, white jumpsuit, white boots, and dark sunglasses. I dressed.

"Put the sunglasses on too. They'll prevent your eyes from burning out."

The man placed his pack in the rear, closed the trunk and then sat behind the wheel while I got in the passenger's seat.

"What's your name by the way?" I inquired.

"I don't have one. I am who I am. But for practical purposes you can call me God. Think of me as your copilot now, Willy."

"Okay."

All of a sudden, the brakes locked, the steering wheel locked, the car hydroplaned, and the radio turned on by itself. A song by Leonard Cohen played: *Hallelujah*.

We flew through the cloud cover, and into another dimension.

"Something might be mechanically wrong with the car," I stated.

"I have everything under control, Willy. Let's see how fast this baby can really go. Fasten your seat belt. At this speed—if I put on the brakes—you'll be thrown into the next universe."

"How fast are we going?"

"Three hundred and fifty million miles per minute."

I checked the odometer, and the gauge was spinning out of control.

"The world is one big ball of confusion today, isn't it, Willy?"

"That's for sure."

"I'm not a happy camper to tell you the truth. Good against evil. Darkness against light. My earth has become poisoned and desecrated. The human race is long over do for a change, and I'm saddened and disappointed by it all. In the beginning, I gave man free will. That may have been a mistake on my part. If today's world continues along the same path, humanity will experience a fall like never before. That's why I've chosen you to help me."

"Why?"

"Because you have a special gift."

"How could I possibly help the Almighty Creator of the Universe?"

"Don't worry. I'll be with you every step of the way. I manage an infinite amount of my own affairs, and it's no simple task keeping everything in balance and in perfect working order. One breath of air is more precious than all the diamonds you have with you. In fact, worth more than all the diamonds on earth. Throughout history, I've been blamed for mankind's miseries and failures. And despite giving everything man could possibly need in life, he still complains it's not enough. Why is that, Willy? I'm perplexed by this."

"I don't know either, Lord."

"If it doesn't bore you much, would you like to hear my plans for the future?"

"Please," I replied while an enormous sun blazed outside the car window; it was so close, I could almost touch it.

"There will be a profound change one day," God stated. "Evil will end, and the good and righteous will rule the planet forever more. Presently. the world's governments and leaders are brainwashing its citizens with television, computer, the internet, and the cell phone. And something coming in the future, called artificial intelligence, will make things much worse. My plan is to end all this. People will have to rely on their own minds to think and act. And relate to one another like decent human beings. Not like robots with metal brains and empty hearts."

"Holy Moses!" I exclaimed while observing the turquoise-green earth from the front windshield. The moon hung high in the distant background.

"Now there's a pretty picture for you," God said while a fiery asteroid sped by us. "Part of my plan is to restore the earth's environment to its original pristine state. As it was, the moment I first created it. You, and every soul on earth will be given two seeds. One is white, and one is red."

"What should I do with them?"

"The white seed is the good seed. The red one is the bad seed. When you return to earth, plant only one. Those who sow the good seed will reap a prosperous harvest of goodness, blessings, and light. Those who sow the bad seed will germinate a weed of eternal evil and darkness."

I looked out the car window, and saw nothing but a blazing fire of light.

"Where are we now?" I inquired.

"We've landed on Mercury. This is where I get off, Willy. Put on my cap. It's the only way you'll be able to breath out here."

I covered my curly red hair with God's multi-colored skull cap. I got out of the car, choked in a breath of air, and then opened the trunk, so God could remove his toolbox and backpack.

He shook my hand. "I appreciate the ride, Willy."

"You're welcome. It was an honor to meet you."

"Likewise."

"How are you going to get to your next destination?"

"Don't worry about me. I have this," God replied as He showed me the cover of a book.

"Hitchhiker's Guide to the Galaxy," I read.

"The revised edition. You can keep the hat. Follow the GPS back to Greece. And just remember, if you ever need me, I'll be in your heart. Or above your head. And one more thing. When you get back on the road, find an empty field and stop. There, you will take off the white clothing and set it on the ground. Toss the red seed with it. And plant the white seed elsewhere. Are my instructions clear to you?"

"Yes, they are."

"Good. Farewell, Willy Maze."

I got in the driver's seat, circled the burning planet of Mercury, passed the 62 moons of Saturn, Alpha Centauri, the freezing winds of the Milky Way, and then the Saab reentered the earth's atmosphere in Greece. The wheels of the car gently bounced upon the asphalt, and I bolted forward.

A few miles down the road, I stopped when I came to an empty field; I walked into it, removed the white clothing, and then piled it on the ground, placing the red seed on top of it. I dug a small hole with my hands, buried the white seed, and then covered it with some dirt. Before returning to the car, I watched a huge fireball brighten up the night sky.

Chapter 22

I rode the brake down a winding mountain highway toward Thessaloniki, a port city in Greece, on the Aegean Sea. There, I slept at a small hotel, soaked in a thermal mineral bath in the morning, and then proceeded south after breakfast.

The air was clammy and hot when I reached Athens. I stopped in front of a dusty Parthenon, where I ate a delicious souvlaki, and then called Johnstone collect from a phone booth. He accepted the charges.

"Hey man."

"Where are you, Willy?"

"Downtown Athens. I'm heading for the ship now."

"Great. I'll see you when you get to the boss' house. Smooth sailing."

"Aye aye, sir."

Off the rocky coast of Piraeus, a city a few miles from Athens, the azure sea glistened while I drove into the port my ship was docked. I calmly gave the customs agent there my boarding pass, ticket, and passport; he saw that my documents were in order, gave them back, and then searched the car, beginning with the trunk; he attempted to open one of the locked suitcases when he received an urgent telephone call from his pregnant wife: *"My water just broke! I had to take a taxi to the hospital. Get here immediately Aristotle."*

With no more ado, the customs agent hung up the phone at his station and waved me and the car up a ramp and into the ship's vehicle hold. I turned off the ignition.

I took out my small suitcase and double-checked the car was secured before searching the ship for cabin number 56. When I found it, the key was in the door.

Inside the small quarters, I washed up from a tiny sink, rested on a chair, and then listened to the ship's hull groan while it chugged away from the slip.

In between decks, I discovered a large room filled with stone and marble busts and statues from the ancient Greek and Roman eras. There was also a varied collection of art, pottery, and ceramic relics from the same time periods. A man in a black pinstripe suit positioned and dusted a bust of Socrates. I approached him.

"Excuse me, sir. Where's the restaurant located?"

"Upstairs, two levels," he replied presenting me with a Hitchcockian angle of his face.

"What are all these statues doing here? Will there be an art exhibition on board?"

"It's going to a museum on the Island of Crete. That'll be our first port of call early tomorrow morning."

"Why aren't the sculptures packed in boxes?"

"Normally that would be the case, sir, but the woman who donated them to the museum, requested they not be. That way there's more chance the sculptures will be damaged before we arrive. They would look more like authentic Greek and Roman art."

"You mean it's all fake?"

The man turned to face me, replying in a disgruntled voice: "I didn't say that."

"Of course not."

The ferry abruptly jettisoned over a liquid buttress, causing a Julius Caesar look-alike to fall on the floor. I helped the museum curator lift the fallen statue upright, noticing its nose and right ear had been smashed, left arm amputated to the shoulder, and its stone-dick broken three quarters off its original length.

The museum curator and I introduced ourselves.

"Thank you for your assistance, Mr. Maze."

"You're welcome, Mr. Serling."

"You can call me Rod."

"Well, I think I could use a drink. Will you join me?"

"I haven't touched the stuff in years, Mr. Maze."

I found the bar, ordered a dry martini, and then had dinner afterwards.

That night in my miniature stateroom, I undressed and washed in a shower smaller than the refrigerator in my apartment in Amsterdam.

On a narrow bed, I counted my blessings, swallowed a melatonin tablet, and then covered myself with a scratchy wool blanket.

The ship sailed into a storm. And 10-foot waves repeatedly rocked the vessel like a dollar store toy, rising over the crest of a wave and crashing down. Screams from cabins and loud noises from things breaking kept me awake. I tightly held onto a bar on the berth's wall and prayed the ship wouldn't sink. After an hour on the watery rollercoaster ride, the Mediterranean became still; a haunting, yet very welcome contrast.

I had difficulty sleeping after that, so I astral traveled out of my cabin for a little midnight stroll on the top deck. I inhaled the marine air and viewed the constellations above, recognizing one in particular: Canis Major. Orion's hunting dog. The brightest star in the sky. I scaled a surreal staircase to a deck above, and sat at an outside bar, where the ship's captain had a pint of dark beer in his hand, chatting up an attractive lady with jet-black hair. She wore a scintillating diamond necklace, a short leather skirt, and a silken blouse with a low-cut neckline. I couldn't believe my eyes at first: she had a striking resemblance to the scaly-skinned woman I met at the Dragonfly Inn. Marie Antoinette.

I put up a hand to disguise my face; in between my fingers, I secretly observed the captain and the woman next to him. They hadn't noticed me yet. I took a longer look; this time she glanced back at me and whispered into the captain's ear. He kissed her on her briny lips. I turned my head toward the sea for a moment, back to the bar, and the captain was gone. The woman was still sitting there, smiling and staring at me.

"I almost never forget a face. Is that you, Marie?"

"It is. And I always remember a head, Billy. Fancy meeting you here. That was some storm, huh?"

"I thought the ship was doomed," I said. "Hadn't seen you at breakfast the morning after our little swimming rendezvous. You're quite the mystery Ms. Antoinette. Where'd you go? Mr. Kirkland told me there was nobody checked in by your name."

"That's because I was checked in under my real name. Donna Leon. Mr. Kirkland has a little dementia. I left early that morning. The airline needed me to fill in for a pilot who called in sick. I had to fly to Nova Scotia. The return flight was to Athens, so I figured I'd do some Island hopping once I got here."

"That should be fun."

"I'm hoping. Listen, Billy. I really enjoyed our evening together, and I think you're a fantastic lover, but I don't want to commit myself to a serious relationship right now. I'm too busy with my career."

"So, that's it?" I asked. "I have feelings you know."

"I do too. We could be friends. Friends with benefits. Would that work? Let me buy you a drink. Cognac?"

"Yes, thanks."

"Jack, I'll have another red wine, and a cognac for my friend. You never told me the name of the company you work for, Billy."

A familiar looking bartender set a glass in front of me, and I thought for a moment. I made one up: "Amsterdam Unlimited."

"How long have you been with them?"

"A couple years."

"I presume they're based in Amsterdam, Holland?"

"That's right."

We knocked our glasses together and toasted: "To life, Ms. Leon."

"And to our friendship with benefits, Billy."

"Cheers."

"After we finish our drinks—we should go to my stateroom—I have something to show you," the woman said.

"So, how'd you become a pilot?"

"My father flew for the French air force. He inspired me to go into the profession. I'd love to know more about this diamond business you're in, Billy."

"There's no such business," I replied. "It was just a pick-up line."

"Oh, really? We'll see about that."

The woman got off her barstool, grabbed my arm, and she helped me stand.

"What are you doing?" I asked.

"I'm taking you back to my stateroom in first class. It's time we used some of those friends with benefits."

I couldn't argue with that. Besides, I was high as a star. Ms. Leon led me to her cabin; she unlocked the door. Inside, I immediately noticed something tall and covered with a sheet at the head of her bed. I pointed to it.

"What's under there?"

"A guillotine."

I laughed while she withdrew the sheet. Sure enough, it was a guillotine. The sharp steel blade gleamed a purplish-silver in the dream-built light.

"That can't be real. Is this some kind of sick joke?"

"How much you wanna bet—stick your head under there."

"No thanks. What are you doing with that thing?"

"I told you before. I'm Marie Antoinette. The woman who likes to cut off heads? Take off all your clothes, Billy. We're gonna have some wild sex now."

She removed my sweatshirt, unzipped my jeans, and pulled them down to my ankles. I didn't wear any underwear. Yikes!

"Oh, you naughty boy. Tell me where the jewels are, Billy."

"You're looking at them."

I was handcuffed, pushed onto the bed, on my back, and then the woman took off her blouse and bra, but left her sexy leather skirt on. She donned her Marie Antoinette wig, reached for a small whip, and then struck my bare chest twice. I yelled. The mad woman shackled my ankles and flogged my stomach.

"I'm not letting you out of this room until you tell me where the diamonds are."

"There are no diamonds—it was just a make-believe story."

"That's a lie. Are you ticklish?"

"A little."

"Let's see what a little feels like," the woman said as she brushed a peacock feather along my skin.

It tickled quite a bit; I couldn't stop laughing.

"Let's see if you're ticklish down there. Oh my! You are."

"Yes, stop. It's too much! Seriously, Marie. Please. That's driving me nuts!" I said, along with a bout of hysterical laughter.

"I won't stop until you tell me where the diamonds are."

"I told you. There are no diamonds."

"Oh?"

She turned me onto my stomach, positioned my head under the guillotine, and then titillated the skin on my back with the feather.

"Tell me where the diamonds are, or I'll cut off your head. Last chance, Billy. I'll count to ten. One, two, three, four, five, six, seven, eight, nine—"

Chapter 23

"Ten," I said to myself as I returned to my physical body, opened my eyes, and then reached for my head: it was still attached.

I flexed and extended my unshackled wrists and ankles, washed my face, and then dressed for breakfast. I heard a sound like motorboats while sunshine flickered past the glass portal in the cabin.

Two decks above, I prepared a plate off the buffet, and sat at a table where the museum curator was reading a newspaper and steeping a tea bag. Butter melted on his English muffin.

"That was some storm we had last night, huh, Mr. Serling?"

"Indeed, it was, Mr. Maze. Many of my statues fell."

"That was the noise I heard."

"Yes, it turned out to be a successful evening," Mr. Serling mentioned.

"You have a substantial number of pieces to unload."

"We have a large work crew ready. Will you be getting off the ship in Crete, Mr. Maze?"

"No, the port of Haifa."

"I've been there. If you ever get the opportunity—you must visit the Carmel Mountains not far from there. In my opinion, it has some of the prettiest landscapes in the entire world."

"I'll have to put that on my bucket list, Rod. And the best of luck with your museum."

The man took a bite of his English muffin. Just then, a noisy flutter of agitated seagulls hovered about the vessel. They seemed distressed. As the ship slowly waded toward the turquoise waters of Heraklion, Crete's major port, several speed boats appeared out of nowhere, and they swiftly encircled the ship.

I heard a sound like machine gun fire. Plates, cups, and glasses shattered throughout the dining room. Mayhem followed.

"Let's get out of here, Rod!" I told the museum curator while observing a frozen look on his face, as if he had turned into one of his cracked Roman statues. I watched him slump onto the table while blood dripped from his neck. The other passengers and I ran for cover while bullets pelted the bow, stern, and port sides.

The ship's captain announced over the intercom: "Attention all passengers and crew members. We may be under attack by pirates. Everyone go below deck and proceed to your cabin immediately! I repeat. We may be under attack by pirates. Take cover now!"

When I reached the stairs to go below deck, a bullet nearly missed my right ear. I stood on the steps and recalled what God had told me when I traveled through Greece: 'I'll be in your heart, or right above your head.' I closed my eyes, placed my hands over my chest, and called for help.

I heard a voice resonate inside the stairwell: "Don't fear the bullets, Willy. Quickly, get on deck, run to the ship's bow, and then hold onto the railing as tight as you can. When I tell you—open your mouth wide."

I did as I was told, and a hurricane-like wind came out of my mouth and blew one of the pirate vessels into the air; it slammed face-down onto the water. The other boats were given the same medicine, and the obliterated motorboats were rocked by the tide while the pirates' lifeless bodies floated nearby.

Chapter 24

The ship slowly sailed into Haifa, and I prepared to drive the car onto dry land. Ambulances waited at the port while emergency personnel boarded the ship and carried off the dead and injured from the pirate attack.

After the customs agent thoroughly x-rayed the Saab's contents, he stamped my passport and waved me through. Before leaving the port, I looked at my directions and traveled south to Tel Aviv.

When I arrived at my destination, I parked beside an acacia tree on 19 Rehov Mesha-Batya, a street in *Kfar Shalem*, a laid-back Tel Aviv neighborhood where mostly Jewish Yemenite hippies, their families, and their mothers and fathers lived. *Kfar Shalem* is Hebrew, for 'village of peace'.

I got out, stretched my arms and legs, and then removed one of the heavy suitcases from the car. I noticed a woman was walking a large brown Rottweiler.

She wore Nikes, a burgundy jogging suit, an LA Dodger's baseball cap, and looked quite healthy and strong for her age. My guess she was in her early seventies. The woman observed the Saab, and she and her dog approached me. The large canine snarled and displayed its gleaming white teeth.

"Quiet, Yossi!" the woman sternly ordered. "He just wants to play—he's friendly."

Yeah, sure. Yossi looked as if he wanted to eat my arm for lunch.

"*Shalom*. Are you Willy Maze?"

"Yeah, who are you?"

"I'm your boss. Mrs. Ben Gurion. Johnstone told me you had red hair and was driving a blue Saab, so I figured it had to be you. He's inside the house. *Mazel tov,* you made it."

"Thanks. It's nice to finally meet you, Mrs. Ben Gurion."

"Likewise."

"I have the merchandise you ordered. The other suitcase is in the trunk."

"We'll deal with that later. Let's go inside the house—I prepared lunch."

"Good, I'm starving."

I locked the car doors, and the woman and her dog led me past a vegetable garden and up to the front door of a two-story house.

"Your tomatoes look nice and ripe."

"You'll be eating them soon—I put them in the salad—welcome to my home, Willy."

"Thank you."

"You can leave the suitcase in the foyer."

There on the wall, I observed a black and white portrait of David Ben Gurion. The first prime minister of Israel.

"Are you related to Mr. Ben Gurion?"

"He was my second cousin on my father's side. I've lived in this house since he was the prime minister of Israel. Johnny, Willy is here!"

"Hey, you finally made it. Congratulations," Johnstone said as he got up from the kitchen table to hug me.

"Hi, Johnstone. The ship had some technical difficulties."

"No worries, man. You're here. That's all that matters now."

After lunch, Yossi and I retrieved the other suitcase from the car, and Johnstone helped me take the luggage to a light-filled workshop at the rear of the house. Through a sliding glass door, I could see a patio, a table with an umbrella and chairs, and a small rose garden outside. An avocado and a lemon tree grew nearby. Mrs. Ben Gurion was sitting at the table drinking a hot tea. She recently picked some lemons and had filled a wicker basket with the fruit.

Few people knew it, but when she was in her mid-twenties, Mrs. Ben Gurion had survived six hellish months during WW2, in the Treblinka concentration camp. She also happened to be one of the most creative and successful jewelers in the world. From various workshops around Europe and Israel, Mrs. Ben Gurion and her employees designed and crafted all the jewelry. And she donated a good percentage of her profits to help deprived children and fund the building of schools, orphanages and hospitals in some of the poorest countries on the planet. As well as providing money for the reforestation of land in Haiti, Brazil, and Africa.

The woman got up from the table outside, opened the sliding glass door, and entered her workshop.

"Let's see what we got here, Willy," the woman spoke while handing me a key. "Open one of the suitcases."

When I did, I saw that it was neatly packed with books. My boss removed a hardcovered text, (at least 350 pages thick) tightly wrapped in translucent plastic. I was slightly confused.

"What's this, Johnstone? I risked my life for smuggling books?"

"That's how the jewels are hidden," he stated.

"In a book?"

"Mrs. Ben Gurion will explain everything," he said.

I watched while my boss took a razor knife and carefully removed the plastic from the book's cover. I read the title on the dust jacket: *If Frogs Could Fly*, by E.B. Mendel."

"Have you read it?" Mrs. Ben Gurion asked.

"No. What's it about?"

"An expedition team searches for a lost tribe of Israel in the rainforest of Peru. They end up becoming victims of a global pandemic. It's a satire. Lots of fun. At least some of it is."

"Sounds pretty interesting, but what about the gems?" I inquired.

The jewelry maker sipped some hot tea then explained: "I invented the plastic the books are wrapped in. It contains a special material which prevents x-rays or anything else from detecting what's hidden inside the text. It's completely foolproof."

"Wow! How'd you come up with that idea?" I asked.

"I developed it many years ago when I worked at a plastic factory on Kibbutz Haogen. Open it."

When I turned-over the hardcover, I saw that its pages were hollowed out and filled with plastic bags containing diamonds, gold and silver ring bands, and other precious gems. I opened a bag, picked out a diamond and held it up, so the sunlight passed through it, refracting many colors inside the gem.

"That's really beautiful," I declared.

"It certainly is. You've done an excellent job, Willy."

"Thank you."

"Do you like to read?" My boss inquired.

"I love to read. Never seem to have the time though."

She reached for a paperback version of *If Frogs Could Fly*, sitting on a shelf.

"It's yours. All the pages are intact."

I curiously leafed through the book.

"Thank you."

"You're welcome. Unfortunately, that edition doesn't come with any jewels. But here's an official cashier's check from the Bank of America. I looked at the amount on the check, $200,000, signed by my boss.

"Thanks. I'm retiring from the business, Mrs. Ben Gurion. This was my last job."

"Oh, I'm so sorry to hear that, Willy. Guess all good things end. You're always welcome to visit. Are you going back to Amsterdam?"

"Not right away. I've planned a trip to Egypt to see the pyramids before I return to Europe. It's always been a dream of mine."

"That should be fun," she said. "Just don't speak any Hebrew over there. And tell no one you've been to Israel, or they might kill you. I'm serious."

"My knowledge of Hebrew is quite limited, but I'll definitely follow your advice."

"Good. When are you leaving for Cairo?"

"In three days. I'll probably check into a hotel by the water and spend some quality time at the beach in the meantime."

"You can stay here till you go. I have a spare guestroom, and Johnstone will be here too."

"Thank you, Mrs. Ben Gurion, but I wouldn't want to impose on you."

"I insist. You're my guest."

"All right then."

"Johnstone will show you where you'll be staying. Excuse me, gentlemen, I have some work to do," the woman said while she removed a plastic bag from another book, and examined some pearls inside.

Chapter 25

The next day, Johnstone and I put shorts on over our bathing suits, and we headed to the beach in the Saab. It was a steamy summer afternoon in Tel Aviv; the water was inviting, but only a few people waded close to the shore. That seemed peculiar. We found a spot, put our towels down, applied sunblock, and then baked.

I couldn't stand the heat anymore, so I got up, went into the sea and splashed warm water onto my face, then treaded my pale-skinned body through the surf. It was good to cool off. I swam underwater a few yards, and surfaced for air; upright, a powerful wave crashed into my chest and knocked me off balance. I swallowed some saltwater, and a strong undertow pulled me away from land. My feet no longer touched the granular bottom, immersed in a frightening depth of swirling black water; I thrashed my legs and flapped my arms to keep above the surface. I spotted the faraway beach. And panicked. People appeared miniature-like while I waved an arm in the air and yelled for help. I realized in that moment, *I'd drown if I didn't start swimming soon.* I noted the shoreline, turned over, and then swam the backstroke as hard as I could. Halfway to shore, my arms and legs gave out, and I went under; the last thing I remembered, was seeing something sparkling yellow.

I felt the beach under me while someone pressed down on my chest several times. They gave me mouth to mouth resuscitation; I coughed up water, and then oxygen returned to my lungs.

I regained consciousness and saw a woman kneeling next to me wearing a flashy yellow bikini.

She cried while I inhaled and exhaled.

"Oh, thank God!—you're alive," the woman exclaimed.

"One breath of air is more precious than all the diamonds on earth," I said.

"That's for sure," the blonde-haired woman said while wiping away tears with her arm.

"Why are you crying?"

"Because I thought you were dead."

"You saved me from drowning?"

"Yes."

"What's your name?" I asked while reaching for her hand.

"Annie."

"I'm Willy."

A tanned and muscular Israeli lifeguard hurriedly ran over to question the woman: "Is he okay?"

"He is now. He just spoke to me."

"Thanks for helping," the lifeguard said.

"You're welcome."

Pale as a ghost, Johnstone arrived at the scene with an ice-cream cone in each hand. "What's the matter with you, man? Didn't you see the signs it was dangerous to swim?"

"What?" I asked, still focused on the pretty blonde in the bikini.

"I said there's a rip tide out there."

"Did you hear me call for help?" I asked the woman named Annie.

"No, but I saw your arms waving in the air, so, I figured you were in some kind of trouble. Here, let me help you sit up," she said while the palm of my hand touched an oval black stone that had the circumference of a goose egg. When she gently pulled me to a sitting position, I took the stone in my hand.

"I thought I was a goner out there."

"You can thank your lucky stars, I know CPR—and I was on my high school swim team. Or you might have been. That's a pretty cool stone—where'd you find it?"

"On the beach, I guess," I replied.

"It looks like an obsidian. It's very unusual to find that kind of stone at the beach."

"Is it? Sorry, this is my friend, Johnstone."

"Hello, Mr. Johnstone."

"Hi. Anyone want ice cream?"

"No, thanks," Annie replied while the frozen desserts dripped from Johnstone's hands.

"Wanna have dinner with me tomorrow night?" I asked the woman.

"I'd love to. But I like to eat late."

"How late?"

"Seven-thirty, eight," Annie replied. "I know a fantastic restaurant in the old city of Jaffa. I could make a reservation for eight fifteen."

"Where ya staying?—I'll pick you up."

"The Hilton on the beach. It's the building right over there."

"I'll meet you by the entrance at seven-thirty. I'll be driving a blue, late-model Saab."

Chapter 26

There must have been at least twenty-five blonde and blue-eyed women come and go from the revolving doors in front of the Hilton, but none looked like Annie.

I was just about to drive away when I noticed an attractive young woman dressed in a tangerine-colored hat and a white cotton sun dress that revealed a pair of trim and well-tanned legs. She lifted the brim on her hat, glanced at the car, and I saw who it was; I got out and opened the door for her.

"Hi, Annie."

"—hope you weren't waiting long, Willy," she said and kissed my cheek.

"No—you're right on time."

"Snazzy wheels."

"It's a rental."

"We can take the coast road. Exit the hotel and go right. Have you ever been to the old city of Jaffa?"

"Never," I replied, as I smelled Annie's perfume and the salt air blow past my nose. "Where we eating?"

"Fitzgerald's. They've got great food. See you brought the stone you found at the beach," Annie said as she picked it up off the console and weighed it in her palm. "Has a really nice feel to it. The Aztec Indians used the obsidian stone for making knives and arrowheads."

"That's interesting. How do you know that?"

"One of my hobbies is studying ancient cultures," she said as she squeezed the stone. "I can feel a warmth."

"Yeah, I felt that too."

In fifteen minutes, we were in the old city of Jaffa.

"Park here. We can walk the rest of the way to the restaurant."

"Is that the old city up there?" I asked while closing the car door.

"Yeah."

I held Annie's hand, and we strolled past a mosque and up a hilly road. At the top, we crossed a square, cut through a cobblestoned alley, and then walked under a rock archway, where we ascended some ancient stone steps which led to a restaurant overlooking the Mediterranean Sea. It all felt like a strange fairytale to me, as I opened a large wooden door, and we entered Fitzgerald's.

"Welcome mates," greeted a pleasant-faced man who spoke with a British accent.

"We have a reservation for 8:15. Annie and Willy," I announced.

"Follow me mates," the host said, escorting us to a table beside a window looking out to a cloudless sky, blood-red sun, and a bluish-green sea. Before we sat, I noticed that Annie had taken the black stone from the car, and was holding it in her right hand.

"This good for you, mates?" the maître de asked.

"It's perfect," I replied. "Sounds like you're from England."

"I am. North London. Been here for forty years, mate. I could never ditch the accent. Enjoy your dinner."

"Thanks. I think it likes you, Annie."

"What?"

"My pet rock."

"Oh," she said, realizing she was still holding it.

A waiter brought us hot bread, hummus, pickles, and olives. He recited the specials, and we ordered. Fish and chips for Annie. Fried chicken and mashed potatoes for me. We asked for a chilled bottle of white wine as well. She set the stone on the table, and the sunlight landed on it.

"Did you think you were going to drown out there?"

"It definitely crossed my mind."

"I'm so happy you didn't," Annie said. "We wouldn't be sitting here right now."

"I know."

I spun the stone around. When it stopped, we both stared at it. It was like some kind of compass; one end pointed toward me; the opposite end pointed east, in Annie's direction. We looked at each other and laughed.

"Should we say a prayer before we eat?" she inquired.

I nodded, held her hand, and we closed our eyes. Annie spoke: "Thank you God for your bountiful blessings. And for giving me a new friend."

"And I'm grateful for my new friend."

"Amen."

"Amen."

I gently squeezed her hand and let go.

We ate some of the appetizer.

"Are you on vacation?" I asked.

"For a couple more days."

"Then what?"

"I'll head back to the Lower East Side of Manhattan where I live and work."

The waiter brought a chilled bottle of wine and opened it; he poured some into two glasses.

"Here's to your health, Willy. And no more swimming in riptides."

"To your health, Annie."

She sensually touched her rose-pink lips to her glass and she drank, leaving a lipstick imprint on the rim.

"What do you do in Manhattan?"

"I'm a professional dancer."

"What kind of dance?"

"Mostly modern. I've done ballet and jazz in the past. What brings you to Israel, Willy?"

"—here on business. At least I was."

"What do you mean?"

"I retired."

"What kind of work did you do?" Annie asked.

"I was a diamond smuggler."

"You're kidding right?" she asked in a disbelieving tone.

"I'm not."

"Sounds pretty adventurous."

"—was at times," I stated.

A Chinese couple paid their bill and got up to leave. The waiter returned, and he replenished our wine glasses.

"Where you from originally?" I asked.

"I was born and raised in Okeechobee, Florida. Then I moved to New York. Where'd you grow up?"

"A place called Newburgh. It's about an hour north of Manhattan."

"I've been through Newburgh. My Uncle Ed and Aunt Tess live in the country a few miles north of there. They own an apple orchard in Marlboro."

"Small world."

"Food smells great," Annie said while she spread a cloth napkin over her lap.

"Can I get you folks anything else?" the waiter inquired.

"Extra lemon. And some Tabasco sauce, please," Annie replied. "So, what were you doing in Amsterdam?"

"I played the clarinet in a professional orchestra."

"Not as dangerous as diamond smuggling," Annie mentioned.

"No."

"Are you still in the orchestra?"

"No, I had to stop. Don't want to talk about it right now."

"We don't have to," she said.

"You want dessert, Annie?"

"I'm full."

"Me too."

"How long are you staying in Israel?" she asked.

"A couple more days. Then I'll go to Egypt to see the pyramids before flying back to Amsterdam. Waiter, can we have the check, please."

"Maybe we can have lunch before you go?" Annie said.

"I'd like that."

As we were about to leave the restaurant, I realized I forgot the stone. When I returned to the candlelit dining room and approached the table, I saw that a circle of glowing violet light surrounded the obsidian rock. I picked it up, put it in my pants pocket, and left.

"You get it?" Annie asked.

"Yeah."

We descended the stone steps and strolled through the moonlit square, listening a few moments while a man played the saxophone. I tossed a dollar into his case before we walked down the hill to the car.

The day before I went to Egypt, Annie and I had lunch at the hotel she was staying at, and we exchanged telephone numbers. We planned on meeting once I returned to the states.

Chapter 27

The morning I departed for Egypt, Mrs. Ben Gurion handed me a small box wrapped like a gift.

"What's this?" I asked her.

"A little going away present. Keep it safe. And promise me you won't open it until you return to Amsterdam."

"I promise. Thank you very much, Mrs. Ben Gurion. And thanks for everything."

"You're welcome, Willy. Does anyone want more pancakes?"

I put my stuff in the car and waved goodbye while Mrs. Ben Gurion stood on the sidewalk with her dog. I sat in the passenger seat of the Saab, and Johnstone drove me to the central bus station in Tel Aviv.

"Safe travels over there, Willy."

"I'll see ya on the flip side, Johnstone."

I purchased a one-way ticket to Cairo, exchanged all my shekels into Egyptian currency at a Bank Leumi, and then boarded a bus. It would be a 12-hour ride to Egypt, most of it through the desert. Thank God for air-conditioned buses! It was 101 degrees in the shade at 7 o'clock in the morning.

Across the aisle from me, I met and befriended two German tourists, Thomas and Rick. Students who were attending college in Berlin. We passed some time in idle conversation.

"What are you guys doing in Israel?"

"Backpacking around the country," Rick answered.

"We just spent three months on a kibbutz by the Sea of Galilee," Thomas added. "Picked a shitload of tomatoes and cucumbers till they were coming out of our ears."

"Ever been to Egypt?"

"We were there a couple years ago," Rick replied.

"Did ya see the pyramids?"

"Yeah."

"How were they?"

"Pretty impressive," Thomas replied.

I opened the novel Mrs. Ben Gurion had gifted me, and I read, until my eyes couldn't stay open any longer.

After several passengers were dropped off and picked up in Be'er-Sheva, (the largest city in the Negev Desert) the scenery got more dramatic. While the modern Egged bus drove through a sharp-turned landscape, I opened my eyes to reddish-brown rock ravines, and a stunning blue sky. I leaned my head on the seat and shut my eyes again.

After some tourists got off in Eilat, the bus eventually reached the Israeli-Egyptian border at Taba.

A couple hours later, I opened a tired eye, and dreamily observed a sober, urban-like landscape interspersed with old and new buildings. The sky appeared more rectangular. Different from the circular sky of the Negev. A bustling oasis. Another planet. A strange alphabet crossed my mind. From the seats ahead of me, I heard people conversing in Arabic. I dozed again.

"Wake up, Willy—we're here," Thomas announced.

The two German students were standing in the aisle of the bus, ready to exit. I nervously grabbed my suitcase and daypack, and exhaustedly followed them off the bus. My adrenaline rushed with feelings of fear and excitement while I planted my sandaled feet on the foreign sidewalk; a dark orange sun lowered into a smog-filled-sky.

From mosques and minarets, the echoing chants of *Allah Akbar* (God is great), reminded me I was no longer in the State of Israel, but inside a country that had a long history of wars and oppression involving the Jewish people, ever since the time of Moses.

I smelled an unpleasant air of exhaust as the bus left.

"Are you coming with us, Willy?" Thomas asked.

"Yeah—how far is it to the hotel?"

"A couple blocks," he answered. "We could take a taxi, but I think it'd be better if we moved our legs after that long ride."

I agreed. The three of us had decided to save money by sharing a hotel room.

We went down a busy street, where we encountered crippled beggars who rested on flattened cardboard boxes on the sidewalk. A man locked eyes with me, and he extended his disfigured arm; I handed him an Egyptian pound, and we proceeded down the street.

"There's an extreme amount of poverty here," Thomas mentioned.

"Yeah, I see."

"Many of the homeless in Cairo have nowhere else to sleep but the cemetery in the city," Rick added.

"That's awfully sad."

"Yeah."

We eventually arrived at a quiet lane shaded by a row of Royal poinciana trees. I read the name on a street sign. *Adley Street.* The Adley Hotel was nestled between a drab apartment building and a structure with a tall white façade designed in the style of an ancient Egyptian temple. I learned later, it was an old synagogue called the *Shaa'ar ha Shamayim,* which means, 'The Gate of Heaven.' It was one of the last surviving synagogues in Cairo, built and completed in 1899, when the first prayer services were held.

I trailed the German tourists up a set of steps and into a minimally decorated hotel lobby. We approached the front desk where a man greeted us: "Welcome to the Adley, gentlemen. Do you speak English?"

"Yes, we do," Thomas answered. "We're together. Do you have a large room with three single beds?"

"How many nights will you be staying, gentlemen?"

"Two. Maybe more."

"Come, I will show you a very nice room."

We followed the hotel clerk into an elevator, up to the fourth floor, into a dismal hallway, along a blue, paper-thin carpet in dire need of a makeover. The man unlocked a door, and he showed us a room: furnished with three skinny beds, two plain lamps with yellowed shades, a drab bathroom with a shower, sink and toilet, a window with a view of Adley Street below, and a television set that didn't work when I turned it on.

After we went downstairs to pay our lodging, the two college students and I washed up and went out for dinner. We walked about a block and a half, and reluctantly agreed upon a poorly lit restaurant. The dining room was congested with loud customers who blew stinky cigarette smoke toward a high ornate ceiling.

Sporting a red fez hat, white apron, dark slacks and white short-sleeve shirt: a tall, pointy-eared waiter seated us, put down menus and then poured ice water into three glasses.

We ordered coffee, and I attempted to decipher the menu in the dim, smoke-filled atmosphere. I got the feeling patrons were staring at us.

Thomas and Rick ordered and shared a whole roasted chicken, but by looking at its bone structure, I argued it was some other type of poultry, perhaps from the pigeon family. I hungrily consumed an innocent plate of olives, hummus, and pita bread.

We paid the bill, left the glumly lit eatery, and then lazily meandered down a sidewalk where Egyptian families window shopped. We returned to the hotel beside the majestic white façade on Adley Street.

Before retiring, I grilled the German guys on how to get to Giza the next day. They planned on visiting the Valley of the Kings; a popular tourist attraction in Luxor, so I would be going to the pyramids alone.

I donned my Superman pajamas, brushed my teeth, and then shut off the lamp by my bed.

Sometime during the night, the ancient sands of Egypt shifted under my feet. I had my clarinet with me as I traveled a long distance back in time. I arrived at the plateau of Giza, a flourishing green oasis where date palms, aloe, banana, and pomegranate trees grew lush. Strange looking men walked shirtless, wore fake beards, unusual pleated white skirts, and turbans. Some of the men haggled deals with one another at the local bazaar while others drank tea and played backgammon outside of cafes. Wearing long dresses that covered or revealed their breasts, young and older women happily shopped in the souk, (the outdoor market).

To fit in with everyone else, I walked like an Egyptian. Sideways. By the entrance to the bazaar, I played my clarinet while observing the lively scene. An audience soon crowded around me to listen. When I ended the melody, they all stood sideways and clapped.

Holding a scepter inlayed with gold and semi-precious stones, wearing a gold robe and red turban, an Egyptian man approached me. "Come—I want you to meet our great king—Pharoah Khufu."

"Who are you?"

"Baalam. The Pharoah's consultant."

"Where is he?" I asked holding the clarinet by my side.

"I will show you. Come."

Baalam escorted me to a marble palace with tall, white columns in the front. In a playing field nearby, strong young men ran races, threw javelins, and wrestled each other. We entered a souvenir shop that sold miniature mummies, pyramids and sphinxes, Nefertiti and Ramses masks, papyrus art, and touristy t-shirts with 'My ancient ancestors built the pyramids' and 'Your mummy is hot, better unwrap her.' I examined a stack of shirts to see if they had any mediums.

"Do not touch!" the turban wearing man snapped.

I took my hand off a shirt, and he led me to Pharoah Khufu's chambers; his weirdly attired emissaries and charcoal-skinned attendants followed.

In a lavishly decorated room, Pharoah Khufu proudly sat on a gold and gemstone throne while his black breasted Hebrew slave girls painted his toenails, and fed him, nuts, grapes, watermelon, and dates.

The fake-bearded king summoned his slave girls to stop their pampering and leave.

When the Pharoah saw my odd-looking superhero pajamas and multi-colored skull cap, he sat sideways and laughed. "Who is this pathetic excuse for a court jester, Baalam?"

"He wants to see the pyramids, oh great Pharoah. I found him playing music in the bazaar. On his strange sounding trumpet."

"What is your name?" the Pharoah inquired.

"Willy Maze. Your highness."

Pharoah Khufu tugged on his fake chin hair and called on one of his Israelite slave girls to cool him with a large hand fan.

"Play me a tune first. If I like what I hear, you shall see my pyramids. If not, you will be castrated. And become my personal eunuch!"

At that moment, I knew I had to play my absolute best. I breathed in air and blew into the clarinet, filling the palace with a sweet sound. The pharaoh appeared entertained, yet confused.

"What is this strange music you play?"

"It's called jazz, your highness."

"Jazz?"

"Yes. Benny Goodman wrote it."

"I like it. You have proved yourself. Come, Benny Goodman. I will show you to my pyramids now. But first, I must see that you can walk like an Egyptian."

I did what he requested, and he was impressed. Once I actually got the hang of it, walking like an Egyptian was quite fun. *Who knew?*

While the casbah rocked, the Pharoah and I went outside, and stood beneath a broiling sun, where thousands of men were beaten and whipped by Egyptian taskmasters, forcing them to do all kinds of rigorous labor; some were charged with mixing materials to make bricks all day. Others worked rope pulleys, levers, and muscle to move stone blocks that weighed a ton. Women slaves carried bread and water buckets throughout the worksite for the starved and sun-burned workers.

"Who are all these people?" I asked the pharaoh.

"My Hebrew slaves, Benny Goodman."

"It looks like they're being worked to death."

"What's wrong with that? They're building me my great monuments. One day when I die, I'll be buried inside the biggest pyramid. That one over there. The great pyramid of Giza!"

"How sad," I said under my breath.

I also saw pharaoh's legions doing something by the Nile River; they were throwing male Israelite babies into the water to drown them. I watched the sea turn red.

It became night, and I heard cats wail underneath the moon and stars.

Wearing multi-colored robes and tall conical hats, Pharoah's magicians brought me inside the great pyramid, and into a large theater filled with empty seats. I sat, was handed popcorn, and a movie came on the screen. It was about the history of how the world began, and how it ended. At the conclusion of the film, I got up and passed through a bewildering labyrinth of secret pathways. I went up the geometric structure, went down, up again, down a thousand times, to the left, to the right, around and around, exited one chamber filled with mummified bodies, then entered another filled with useless relics. Lost, till I found myself in the pinnacle of the pyramid, where a blinding gold light shined to the outside; I squinted through a triangular-shaped window and observed the sun, the sky, and the whole universe. I plum forgot where I was. Who I was. I fell through a hole in the floor and landed in another chamber, where Pharoah's mortuary attendants washed and prepared dead bodies with embalming fluid; everything stunk. As I observed a row of cadaverous mummies against a wall, I begged God to be released from the tomb.

"I will prepare him for the afterlife now," one of the mortuary workers said.

"I'm not dead. Hello. I'm not dead!"

My defense was not heard; the undertakers smashed my clarinet, stripped me naked, sponged me with the formaldehyde, and then wrapped my body with strips of white cloth. They carried me out of the parlor, and onto an Egyptian sailboat that floated down the sanguine Nile. I tried yelling for someone to save me, but my supplications were muffled behind the mummy wrap.

"—get me out of here!"

I heard a foreign voice, "What's the matter, Willy?"

A light shined in from the hotel window, and I opened my eyes.

"Are you okay?" Thomas asked while I released myself from a tangled bed sheet.

"Yeah. Just had a crazy dream. What time is it?"

"Seven. We're going for breakfast—coming with us?"

"Let me take a quick shower."

"Hurry . . ."

Chapter 28

A modern subway in Cairo stopped; the door opened, and then early morning commuters rudely pushed me from behind, ejecting me onto the station platform.

Outside, several taxi drivers waited inside their idling vehicles; a few of them announced through their open windows:

"Taxi, sir?"

"Taxi, mister?"

"Taxi, my friend?"

"Yeah, I need a taxi," I said to one of the drivers.

"Please, get in."

I thanked him in Arabic, *"Choukran."*

"Where you going?" the driver asked me.

"Giza—the pyramids. How much is it?"

"Yes, Giza. I will take you. Don't worry. You pay after. Relax."

I sat next to another rider. Soon after, someone else got in the cab, and I was squeezed in between.

As if the cab drivers were on the starting line for an Indianapolis 500, a dust cloud formed after they simultaneously bolted to a dissonance of roaring engines, screeching tires, blaring radios, and honking horns. Stop signs, traffic lights, and traffic rules were seldom obeyed in Cairo, because there were none.

The cabby got on a ramp for the highway, and we passed many impoverished Cairo suburbs. Forty-five minutes later, I viewed Giza's hazy, but colorful skyline.

The driver parked his dented Mercedes in a dusty old neighborhood square. I paid him, stood on the sidewalk, and then curiously scanned the local scenery. I walked over to a shaded bench, where I gathered my scattered thoughts: *What on earth are you doing in this strange place, Willy? I wonder where the pyramids are.* I drank from my water bottle, ate a banana, a handful of dates, and an orange.

I rose from the bench, walked a short distance, and then bumped into a young Egyptian man.

"Do you speak English?" I asked.

"A little."

"How do I get to the pyramids?"

"You want tour of pyramids? I am excellent tour guide. My name is Mohamed. Like the prophet."

"Yeah, I'd like a tour."

"Come with me. First, we go to papyrus museum and gift shop."

"After I see the pyramids."

"As you wish, my friend."

With my Walgreen's throw-away camera in hand, the well-tanned Egyptian man led me to the end of a pebbled street, up a short incline of sand, past a building, beyond another mound of sand, and there they were: several yards in front of us, larger than life, a golden yellow sun glistened over them: the Great Pyramids of Giza. A large, medium, and small. Nearby, the Sphinx pensively crouched in a state of blissful oblivion. The tour guide interrupted my contemplation.

"You want horse or camel?"

"For what?"

"Tour of pyramids."

I thought for a moment.

"A horse will be fine."

"Wait here. I come back ten minutes."

The tour guide returned, saddled atop a tall black stallion while gripping the reigns of another horse alongside him: a majestic brown mare. He climbed down from his saddle, helped me onto my ride, and we cantered out into the silent desert.

"Can we go inside the pyramid?" I asked while we slowly approached the tallest one.

"Not allowed today—Ramadan."

"Oh."

I wasn't too disappointed, especially after having the bizarre mummy dream the night before.

In order to capture a more panoramic view, we trotted farther away from the giant monuments.

"How do you make the horse go faster?"

"Like this," he replied while gently kicking his heels against the horse's flank.

Guess I kicked her harder than necessary, because she bolted in a full gallop over a flat stretch of sand. I couldn't stop the horse, and I suddenly found myself in the Kentucky Derby. My heart pumped fast while I balanced myself in the saddle, gripping the camera and pulling on the reigns. I screamed for Mohamed to help me. The horse slowed down when she anticipated a steep-angled sand dune. We climbed the sand ramp, went no farther, and then carefully walked in reverse down the incline. Thank God, the animal was experienced enough to keep its balance and not fall backwards, or else I might have broken my neck, or been crushed underneath its huge body. My tour guide trotted over to assist me.

"Are you okay my friend?"

"Yeah, I just didn't want to get here that fast."

He laughed, but I wasn't intending to be funny.

"You take picture of pyramids now," he said.

The tour guide photographed me on the horse with the pyramids and the Sphinx in the background. I snapped a few images, and we safely headed back to our starting point.

After my grand tour of the Sphinx and the three geometric wonders of the world, I paid my guide, spent two hours inside the airconditioned museum, where I drank an ice-cold Coca Cola and purchased some papyrus-art souvenirs from the gift shop before returning to the neighborhood square.

The late afternoon sun was setting while I watched a commotion of people and vehicles rapidly disappear from the plaza. A man sitting in a dirty gray Mercedes was left behind, and the place I had come to hours earlier, now looked like a ghost town in the *wild West*. All it needed was some thistle and tumbleweed. The man got out of the Mercedes to light a cigarette, and I asked him if he could take me back to Cairo.

"I visit my family. Ramadan," he said.

"No more taxis or buses?"

"No," he replied, about to get into his car and drive off.

"—wait! —if you take me to Cairo—I'll pay you double the fare."

He took a drag from his cigarette and thought for a moment.

"Get in."

He drove away from the square, and it was dark all of a sudden. He only went a couple minutes down a cobblestone street, stopped, and then turned off the Mercedes engine in front of some brick houses. I felt a foreboding.

"What are you doing here?"

"Say hello to my family. Come—we drink tea."

I grew anxious. "I'll wait in the car."

"They are nice people. Come. It's my family."

I glanced at the dark and empty street. *What choices did I have?*

I opened the car door, got out, and a voice in my head told me it was safe for me to go inside the house. While another voice said: 'If you follow him inside, you'll be killed'. *I could walk away, but I'd have no idea where to go, or what to do.* I stood by the car and heard the taxi driver say again: "*Yalla*—we drink tea."

He wasn't taking no for an answer. I followed him to the front door; he knocked; the door opened, and then he happily greeted a woman who had two small children by her side. She returned the greeting, and he said something else to her. She looked at me with broad discerning eyes.

I smiled and said hello.

We were invited in.

While we stepped through the doorway and into a lighted foyer, I reminded myself not to speak any Hebrew, recalling what Mrs. Ben Gurion had warned me.

I followed the man into a living room, where two men sat and four kids watched television. The children curiously looked up, and the woman ordered them to play somewhere else. She darkened the television.

I put on my friendliest face, and the taxi driver introduced me to the two men. I shook their hands.

Each one announced their name:

"Ibrahim."

"Yusaf."

"Nice to meet you. I'm Willy. *Allah Akbar.*"

They mumbled back, *"Allah Akbar."*

I was invited to sit on a cushion on the floor, and one of the men briefly told the woman who answered the door something in Arabic. She acknowledged him and left.

The men looked at me again, and I hoped the tea would be served soon, so I could return to Cairo. They scrutinized my western appearance, and I concealed my apprehension behind it.

"Where you from, Willy?" the more inquisitive gentleman asked.

"The United States. New York."

"New York?" he slowly asked as if it was on a different planet.

"Yeah."

"Are you Jew?" the other man inquired.

Without hesitation, I replied: "No, I'm a Christian."

I don't know what his thoughts were after telling him that, but they asked nothing more. Uncomfortable, I continued to hide the fear that grew in my chest.

The woman brought in a tray with glasses of tea and lemon wedges on it.

After everyone drank the tea, the woman appeared with bottles of beer.

To be polite, I drank one.

Meanwhile, one of the men opened a small packet of hashish, and he rolled a joint with loose tobacco.

I got really stoned. And soon after that, I became paranoid. And more intent on leaving.

Fifteen minutes later, the woman of the house returned, carrying a platter of meat, I had no interest in eating. They urged me to have some, but I told them I was a vegetarian. I politely nibbled on some pita bread and hummus.

By now, the guy who was supposed to drive me back to Cairo had become too intoxicated to go anywhere.

I worried about my situation; one of the men had taken a liking to me.

What did I get myself into? Shit!

I pleaded for someone to give me a ride back to Cairo, but everyone politely smiled and spoke Arabic among themselves.

I was offered another beer and declined with a 'no thanks' that accidently slipped out of my mouth in Hebrew. Nobody caught it, but me. *Jesus, that was close,* I thought.

Before long, my designated taxi driver had fallen into an even deeper stupor. Fast asleep.

I looked above and silently prayed. *Please God, help me get out of here tonight.*

I persuaded one of the more sober Egyptian men to give me a ride back to Cairo. He said we would leave in a few minutes. That turned into a half hour.

A voice told me all the lights in the house would go off momentarily; when they came back on, my new driver would get up to leave, and I should follow him. The house became quiet and pitch black. Moments after, the lights came on, and my driver was standing and smiling.

I thanked my hosts for their kind hospitality while my driver said goodbye to his family.

We exited the house, got into a car, and a group of children excitedly ran up to my window and asked me for *baksheesh* (money). I gave them a few Egyptian notes and rolled up the window. They happily waved goodbye, and I was relieved to be on my way.

The man drove off. A few minutes later, he stopped at a brightly lit convenience store and parked.

I felt that foreboding again. *This is where I'll be killed.* I thought.

"I buy cigarettes," he said.

I waited in the front seat, fearfully staring at the storefront window.

The man appeared shortly after, unwrapping a pack of smokes. He offered me one, and I declined.

He backed out and left.

I breathed again.

Forty minutes down the road, I saw the gleaming amber lights of downtown Cairo.

"Where is hotel?" the man asked.

I reached into my pocket for the book of matches I had taken from the front desk before leaving in the morning; it had the telephone number, and the name and address of the hotel. I couldn't find it. I searched my pockets and my day pack. *Did I accidentally lose the matches while I was riding the horse? What's the name of the hotel?* My mind drew a blank. I tensed up.

"Where is hotel?" the driver inquired once more.

I wiped a bead of sweat from my forehead.

"I don't know."

The silent driver patiently roamed the empty streets while I kept an eye out for the lodging.

I glanced out the window and saw we were leaving the city altogether.

"Wait—where you going? Go back," I sternly spoke.

He made a U-turn and drove into the center of Cairo once more.

Please, God, help me find the hotel. Please God, help me find the hotel. That's all I focused on while the driver turned onto another road, searching for a hotel and street with no name. When the situation seemed hopeless, I noticed a familiar looking building with a majestic white façade.

"Slow down—this looks," I said while seeing two soldiers standing guard in front of an illuminated white building. "This is it, here! Stop."

I handed the driver a large Egyptian note and told him to keep the change. I viewed the building's white portico and raised my camera, about to take a picture when one of the soldiers saw me and strictly ordered: "No pictures!"

I complied, and walked around to the entrance of the Adley Hotel. By coincidence, the two German tourists were coming down the stairs—the same time I was going up.

"We were worried about you, Willy. How were the pyramids?" Thomas inquired.

"Amazing, but you're never gonna believe what happened to me tonight."

"We're getting something to eat—you can tell us on the way," Rick said.

All I thought about that night was getting out of Cairo as soon as possible.

In the morning, I walked along Adley Street, went inside the first travel agency I saw, and then booked a flight to Amsterdam for the following day.

Chapter 29

Back in Amsterdam

At 9 o'clock in the morning, I got off the train from the airport and walked onto the promenade at Central Station, where Guillermo, an Argentinian solo jazz virtuoso on the electric guitar, had tuned and warmed up his pig-nose amplifier. I smiled, listened a few moments and then dropped a Dutch coin into his case before catching a tram to the Museumplein.

I stood in front of Mrs. Vanderkughel's apartment building, got my keys out, and briefly glanced at the pyramid in the sculpture garden before going inside.

I retrieved my mail, passed Lotty's old flat, and then climbed the staircase to my apartment. The telephone rang just as I opened the door. I hurried in, and picked up the receiver.

"Annie?"

"Who's this?" the person on the other end inquired in a familiar but faraway voice.

"It's Willy."

"Hi, Willy, it's your mother."

"Hi, Mom. Sorry, I was expecting a call from someone else."

"I haven't heard from you in two weeks. I thought something happened to you."

"I've been busy with the diamond business, Mom—how's everything there?"

"Not so good. Your father had open-heart surgery a few days ago. Don't you check your messages?"

"Oh, my God. I was out of the country—how's he doing?"

"So, so. He came home from the hospital yesterday. He's sleeping right now. Who's Annie?"

"Someone I met on the beach in Tel Aviv. She saved my life."

"That was nice of her. How's the jewelry business?"

"I don't work for them anymore."

"What do you mean?"

"I quit."

"That's too bad—you were making good money. What are you going to do now?"

"I'm planning on coming back to the states. Maybe find some music work on Broadway again."

"I have to go, Willy—your father needs something."

"Tell him I wish him a speedy recovery. Love you, Mom."

I hung up the phone, brought my suitcase in from the hall, and then kicked off my shoes. I sat on the couch, reached into my shirt pocket and removed the gift Mrs. Ben Gurion had given me. I tore off the wrapping, and opened a small-hinged box. There was a diamond inside. And suddenly, I watched an ethereal gold light flood the entire living room.

Chapter 30

While friends, neighbors and relatives sat shivah (mourned) in my mother's living room, I sullenly watched mom's first cousin, Sonny, the vegan long-haired yoga instructor from Sedona, Arizona, sit cross-legged in a corner. He was dressed in white, and quietly chanting to himself: "*Om shanti. Om shanti.*"

When Sonny had arrived at the house, he came bearing gifts. A fashionable leather handbag for mom, and a brown felt cowboy hat for me. It was a little corny but I liked it; it was different. I wore it in the house. My relatives thought that was a little strange, although Sonny was pleased.

After I heard the news, my father had died, I was in such a hurry to pack and book a flight to JFK and then Newburgh, I forgot to put the piece of paper with Annie's phone number on it, back inside my wallet. I spoke to her the day before I left Amsterdam.

I asked myself: *Why didn't I give Annie my mom's number? Stupid me!* I had my ex-landlady's number, so I went into the privacy of the kitchen, took off the western-style hat, and then phoned her.

"Mrs. Vanderkughel?"

"This is she."

"Hi, it's Willy—I'm sorry to bother you at this hour—but I need a big favor."

"What is it, Willy?"

"I left an important note on the table by the couch."

"I threw it in the trash. I did a thorough cleaning of the flat yesterday. I'd look for you, but the garbage was picked up this morning."

"Oh . . . darn it."

"Sorry about your father, Willy."

"Thanks."

I despondently hung up the phone, placed the black stone on the kitchen table and then spun it; it stopped, and one end indicated south. I had a strong feeling Annie was in Manhattan. The Lower East Side, where she said she lived and worked. I put the cowboy hat on. Just then, my mother walked into the kitchen with an empty food platter.

"Why aren't you eating, Willy?—there's plenty of food in the living room."

"I will. I had to make a phone call."

"What's with the hat?"

"Sonny gave it to me."

I rejoined my father's grieving relatives, friends, and neighbors in the living room while my Aunt Trudy stuffed her face with gefilte fish and creamed herring, her husband packed a plate with smoked white fish and chopped liver, and my cousin Mindy chomped on a tall salami sandwich on a Kaiser roll. I went over to the catered smorgasbord and served myself some tuna salad on a slice of rye bread without seeds, and a potato knish. Sonny stood beside me, filling a plate with tofu and bean sprouts drizzled with soy sauce.

"See ya like the hat," he said.

"Yeah, it's pretty cool. Thanks again. So, how's the yoga business doing in Sedona?"

"It's booming. A lot of hot chicks in my classes. I get laid almost every other night."

"That's nice."

"You gonna take over your father's deli?"

"I don't know yet."

Chapter 31

Two day later, on the first of August, I borrowed my father's old blue Chevy, opened a bank account in the Vails Gate Savings and Loan, and then deposited the $200,000 check I had in my wallet since leaving Israel.

After my business at the bank, I purchased a decent quality hiking compass at the army-navy store on Broadway, and then drove across the Newburgh-Beacon Bridge. I used the compass in conjunction with the black stone I found at the beach in Tel Aviv, when I first met Annie. It even came with a nifty leather carrying case that clipped onto my belt.

I stopped at the bridge toll booth, paid a dollar, and then headed for the train station in Beacon, where I purchased a round-trip ticket to mid-town Manhattan.

An hour later, the train ambled through a long dark tunnel near Grand Central while I roughly planned my itinerary in the grimy city of dreams.

The train squealed to a stop; I took an escalator up to the colossal main concourse at the station, where elongated beams of sunlight shone in from long rectangular windows. Morning commuters darted in and out of entrances and exits, running to and from trains, into cabs, buses, or descending dirty staircases leading to odorous subway stations.

In the middle of the concourse, I stood by a four-faced clock at the info desk and asked the location of the New York Public Library.

Exiting Grand Central, I stepped onto a broad, blue stone sidewalk while a blonde woman who looked like Annie, passed in a blur of crowded pedestrians. I thought it was her and called out her name. They disappeared.

In a graffiti-filled and urine-smelling subway station, I purchased a token, and held my nose closed while waiting on the platform for an approaching train. I boarded a subway car, found a seat beside a blue-collar worker who was reading a newspaper and checking the numbers on a lottery ticket.

I got off at the 5th Ave and 42nd Street stop, went upstairs, and then walked a block to the library.

Inside the main reading room, I found the newspaper rack and grabbed the Wednesday edition of the New York Times, opening it to the leisure and arts section and browsing the pages where the Broadway shows and dance performances were listed.

I heard a child ask nearby. "Can we get ice cream, Mommy?"

"Annie, stop it," a woman replied from behind a bookshelf.

I quickly got up from the table to see where the voice had come from. It was a mother disciplining her young daughter. I watched them while I took a book off the shelf and pretended to read it.

"Annie, you have to be quiet in the library. We'll get some ice cream later."

The little child started crying.

I put the book back and returned to where I was sitting. I jotted down all the information I could find about venues with dance performances and Broadway musicals. I unfolded a map of Manhattan, placed the black stone on it, and spun it. When it stopped, I put the compass over it; the needle pointed south to the intersection of Broadway and Park Row. I gathered everything and left for the subway. There was a theater down there Annie could possibly be dancing in.

At the end of Park Row and Broadway, I stood in awe for a few moments as I looked up at the tallest skyscrapers in the world: the twin towers of the World Trade Center. I asked an elderly woman if she knew where the Park Theater was. She told me it burned down years ago.

I resumed my quest along a drizzling Ann Street, crossed Broadway and Church, till I ran right into the

World Trade Center entrance. I took the elevator 110 floors to the roof observatory, where I viewed the great metropolis and beyond. A long black cloud appeared, and the heavens opened. The rain only lasted a minute, and I was suddenly struck by an uneasy feeling after two large passenger jets grazed the overcast skyline. I faced the east and prayed: *God, help me find Annie. She must be down there somewhere.* I entered the elevator once more.

In the lobby of the skyscraper, I sat at a table, unfolded the map, and then spun the black stone. The compass directed me to the Lower East Side, 205 Houston Street to be exact.

I took a cab there, got out, and then looked up at Katz's red and white neon sign. I entered the kosher-style deli and was seated at a table next to three older men who were drinking coffee and eating sponge cake. A lanky younger man with a crazy looking hairstyle, sat at the table in front of me. I glanced at his lunch plate; it looked like he was eating a hamburger deluxe.

"*Bon appetite,*" I wished him.

"What the fuck is that supposed to mean, man? I don't speak your language."

"It's French for have a good appetite," I replied. "Sorry, I didn't mean to be nosey."

"That's okay. I was only joking. Excuse my New York humor."

"You look very familiar," I said.

"I'm Cosmo, from Seinfeld."

"Kramer? I thought it was you. My name's Willy. Willy Maze."

"Hey man, I thought you were black."

"I'm not the baseball player. It's spelled M-a-z-e."

"Oh," he grunted, then took another bite of his burger.

"Are you really from Seinfeld?"

"Why, you don't believe me? Watch this."

He got up, walked past my table, and slid on the floor, performing his famous Kramer-like entrance and nervous-like gesture with his hands.

"What do you think of that?" he asked.

I laughed. "That's Kramer alright. You come here often?"

"Almost every day. In between shows and rehearsals. I live down the street," the actor replied. "Why do you ask?"

"I'm looking for a woman who lives in the neighborhood."

"What's her name? —I know everyone around here."

"Annie Rose," I replied. "She's about 5'6", fair skin, blue eyes, long wavy blonde hair, and a body like Marylyn Monroe. She's a dancer."

"What kind of dancer?"

"Modern, I think."

The man who said he was on Seinfeld, scratched his head a few moments, pushed away his plate, drank some coffee, and then made a hand gesture like a light bulb had turned on above his head.

"I know the woman you're looking for! I've seen her in here before. She dances in a place down the street."

"Where?" I inquired.

"A burlesque theater called New York New York. Wow! Man, what a beauty. Talented young woman. Great legs."

"When did you last see her dance?"

"About a month ago."

"Where's this New York New York?"

"On Delancey Street. I'll take you there after you eat."

"Are you sure it won't be an inconvenience for you?" I asked.

"I don't have to be on the set till 6 o'clock."

"Hey, could I get your autograph?" I asked the man from Seinfeld.

I quickly ate, paid mine and Kramer's bill, and the two of us walked out of Katz's and hailed a taxi to Delancey Street. The cabby dropped us in front of a red brick facade. The New York New York burlesque theater. The advertisement displayed: magic shows, nude male and female dancers, and comedy on Monday nights.

"Let's see who's performing today," Kramer said as we approached the ticket window.

Inside, a puffy faced man inquired, "Hi, Bill. Can I help you?"

"Who's dancing today, Sam?"

"Betty Boop is on stage right now. Then Candy, Sally, Honeysuckle, and Blaze. Bernie and Joe are scheduled for the late evening shows."

"Annie Rose isn't dancing today?" the guy named Kramer inquired.

"She quit a few days ago."

"Damn. Excuse me," I said to the guy on the other side of the ticket window.

"Yeah, what do you want, kid?"

"This Annie who quit. She have blue eyes, wavy blonde hair and a great figure?"

"Why—you a cop—or something?"

"No, a friend of hers."

"Yeah, she's got wavy blonde hair. And eyes bluer than the ocean. Any more questions?—you're holding up the line—kid."

"Just one more question. Those dancers, Bernie and Joe—they're women, right?"

"Listen, pal. How many women do you know named Bernie, or Joe?"

"None."

"Good. You fellas gonna buy tickets or not?"

"I'll pass."

"How 'bout you, Bill?"

"Give me a ticket for Candy's show, Sam."

"Hey, I thought you said your name was Kramer," I said.

"Man, I tell that to everybody I meet. Pretty good impersonation, right?"

Chapter 32

Four days later

Once the alarm clock jarred me out of bed, I prayed, did some hatha yoga, showered, and then dressed for another long day in Manhattan; it was a sunny, yet cool mid-September morning. I put on my cowboy hat, came downstairs and poured myself a coffee. My mother was sitting at the kitchen table.

"Morning."

"Morning, Willy. What time did you get home last night?"

"About midnight."

"Any luck finding Annie?"

"No."

"Make yourself some breakfast. I'm really sorry, Willy. Wish I could do more to help you. You'll find her. Remember what your father used to say?"

"What's that?"

"If there's a will, there's a way. I've talked to a man who's interested in buying the deli."

"That's great. I'm really glad you quit smoking, Mom."

"I am too. You're not gonna eat any breakfast?"

"I'll get something on the way. Don't wait up for me. I'll probably be back late," I said while grabbing the black stone and the car keys.

"Good luck, Willy."

"Thanks. See ya later."

I filled up the gas tank on Windsor Highway, travelled route 32, and then veered onto the bridge while the sun gleamed from the east, making the caps on the Hudson River glisten like silver and copper coins. I pulled down the sun visor, turned on the news, paid the toll, and then took the exit for the Metro station in Beacon.

I held the smooth black stone and looked out the train window. I leaned my head on the glass, closed my eyes and thought about Annie, picturing her suntanned face, her billowy blonde hair, and pleasantly shaped figure. When I placed the stone up to my nose, I could almost smell the perfume she wore the night we had dinner together at the restaurant overlooking the sea.

The train chugged down the tracks and snaked alongside the brilliant green Hudson, past Breakneck Ridge, the steep granite cliffs of Cold Spring, West Point, Garrison, and Bear Mountain.

I kept on seeing these mysterious images in my mind; leftover from a dream I had the night before. A man tossing an apple in the air, a headless horseman, a yellow dog chained to a tree, a woman wearing a long black dress, and a bearded old man sitting on a rock and starring at the ground, like he was Rip Van Winkle, in the Legend of Sleepy Hollow.

When I opened my eyes, the train was smoking into Tarrytown station, where some of that legend supposedly took place. Through my window, I watched morning commuters prepare to board. Next stop: Irvington, then Dobs Ferry, Hastings, Yonkers, Riverdale, the Bronx, and Harlem. Before I knew it, I was in Grand Central.

I rode the escalator up to the spacious station hall, and went outside and stood on the Manhattan sidewalk. A public transit bus had stopped in front of me, and I watched while a blonde woman boringly stared out the window of the bus. *God—she looked just like Annie!* I waved to her just as the bus drove away. On the back of it, was another one of those tobacco ads: A cowboy on a horse. *Welcome to Marlboro country.*

I quickly went along the busy sidewalk; in the direction the bus had gone, ending up in Times Square, on 42nd Street, where some prostitutes were gathered by a public bus stop.

"Excuse me, ladies," I said. "I'm looking for a pretty blonde woman who was on a bus—have you seen her get off at this stop by any chance?"

One of the women in the group looked at me as if I was nuts. She replied: "The bus just left mister. And I didn't see any blondes get off. But I can get you off for fifty dollars, sugar. How 'bout it?"

Ignoring the businesswoman's offer, I raised my arm for a cab; it stopped; I opened the yellow door and got in.

"Where to, pal?" the driver asked while he turned on the meter.

"Radio City Music Hall."

"Going to see the Rockettes?"

"No, I'm looking for somebody."

"Aren't we all," the cabby said while passing another billboard that advertised cigarettes.

Then it suddenly dawned on me: *Marlboro man. The country. Uncle Ed.*

"Life's a puzzle, isn't it, pal," the cabby stated.

"What?"

"You ever get to thinking why it twists and turns in so many directions? If you could count them, it'd probably be in the millions."

"Marlboro!" I shouted from the back seat of the taxi.

"What the fuck is wrong with you, pal? You almost gave me a heart attack."

"Sorry. Take me to Grand Central."

"I thought you wanted to see the Rockettes."

"Some other time."

Chapter 33

That same day

The night we had dinner together in Jaffa, Annie mentioned her aunt and uncle owned an apple orchard in Marlboro, New York, so I figured they would know something about her whereabouts.

The taxi dropped me at Grand Central, and I ran to where my train was waiting; it departed at noon.

I closed my eyes, and didn't open them until the train rolled north into Beacon. The station clock there showed it was half-past two. It was cooler and windier upstate; the sky had grown older, and a drearier color gray than Manhattan. I unlocked the car, put on a sweatshirt, and then left the station.

The Hudson whipped up a noticeably strong cross current as I drove over the bridge (Interstate 84) and into Newburgh. I got on Route 9W north, left the town, and then not long after, coasted through the tiny hamlet of Marlboro.

I passed several orchards, Milton's Hardware and Building Supply, a small farm market, and the Ship Lantern Inn high atop a hill facing the river.

I made a U-turn, pulled into the farm market, and went inside. Grateful Dead music played from a speaker on an empty apple crate while an elderly woman weighed a bag of fruit on a large metal and glass scale. She wore a ski cap atop her white hair, a long gray apron over a brown sweater. The woman appeared tired as she glanced up at my cowboy hat and smiled. *If her eyes could speak.*

"Hello."

"Good afternoon. Can I help you?"

Lost for words, I inhaled the strong scent of apples.

"Have any Golden Delicious."

"How much do you need? I only have one box left."

"Four pounds."

The woman went to the back and bagged some yellow apples from a crate. She returned and put it on the scale.

"It's a little over five," she informed me.

"That's okay."

"Three dollars. I'll only charge you for four pounds."

I gave her the cash and asked, "I'm looking for an orchard in Marlboro—it's owned by a husband and wife."

"The country around here is filled with apple orchards, young man. Do you know the name of it?"

"I only know that the farmer's name is Ed."

"A man named Edward Rosenfeld has an orchard in Marlboro. I buy apples from him sometimes. Saw him and his wife at the gas station last week."

"Where's the orchard located?"

"On Old Indian Road. It's called Stonybrook Farm. They live in a big yellow farmhouse up there. There's a brook that runs down beside the road. Real pretty land."

"Is it close by?"

"A few miles southwest of here—I can write down the directions for you."

"That would be great. Thanks."

I bit into an apple while the woman found a pen and paper. She sketched a rough map. Outside, a pack of motorcyclists thunderously drove past, and it was quiet again.

"You'll have to go back into Marlboro to get to Old Indian Road," the woman stated as she handed me the paper with the map and directions.

I thanked her again, studied the little map, put the bag in the car, and then drove south on 9W a few miles.

Willow Tree Road appeared, The Ship Lantern Inn, and a mile and a half more, I approached the intersection of Old Indian Road. I saw it again: this time on a dilapidated billboard in the brush, on the roadside. A man on a horse; his face, head and cowboy hat were missing. I read the words above the headless horseman: **Welcome to Marlboro Country.** *That's the headless horseman I saw in my dream.* I said aloud.

I travelled about eight miles more, passed several orchards, but no Stonybrook Farm. *Maybe I missed it? Maybe the orchard went out of business, and new owners purchased it and changed the name. Perhaps Annie Rose doesn't even exist. And this is all a figment of my imagination.* My thinking frightened me. *Get a hold of yourself, Willy.*

I kept hearing voices as I traveled no faster than 35 mph. I scaled a hill, and a yellow, three-story farmhouse appeared. Plump red apples hung from trees on one side of the road; the apple trees on the other side appeared fruitless and burnt by something. I stopped the car and happily read the words on a square wooden sign: *Stonybrook Farm.* Across the street, I observed a spooky white house with its unpainted wooden window shutters closed tight. A mean and ugly dog was chained to a dead elm tree in the front yard. It angrily barked at me. I smelled somebody burning something beyond the house, and heard horrendous screaming from that direction. I pulled into the gravel driveway at the yellow farmhouse, and parked near an old tractor and a rusted red Buick alongside it; all four of its tires were flat.

I got out, walked to the front door, and rang the bell. I knocked. It didn't look like anyone was home.

A calico cat darted by me and ran into a ramshackle barn. I followed it, and called from the open entrance: "There someone in here?"

The cat meowed next to my leg, and it ran into the orchard; I followed it.

Tall wooden ladders leaned against the trees, and large bins were filled with fruit, ready to be taken to market. I walked to the end of the row, climbed a steep hill, and then viewed the lazy Hudson below. I sang some words of a song I knew well:

> Down by the river the water's runnin' low
> as I wander underneath the trees
> In the park outside of town
> the leaves turned brown and yellow now
> are falling on the ground
> Remembering the way you felt
> beside me here when love was new
> That feeling's just grown stronger
> since I fell in love with you
> *Now we've only got these times we're living in*
> *We've only got these times we're living in . . .*

I hiked the ridge and came to a glade filled with tall mullein, burdock, yellow yarrow flowers, and blueberry bushes. I startled a beaver who sprinted away and vanished down the hill.

Farther along, I came to an old round greenhouse. Even the roof was glass. I pushed open the wooden door, and stood inside. Black soil and empty clay flowerpots were on a worktable and concrete floor. I sat on a stool and rested. The sun would be setting in less than an hour. I wanted to leave, but something kept me there, some sort of energy field.

Down below, an old Ford truck pulled into the driveway of the yellow farmhouse, and it parked beside the old blue Chevy. Passengers and driver looked at the car, wondering who owned the vehicle.

"Whoever it belongs to, they're probably up in the orchard," a man spoke while opening the truck door. "We'll get the groceries in sweetheart—can you go and see what they want? And bring Webster with you. He needs some exercise."

While I rested in the round greenhouse on the top of the hill, I removed the black stone from my pocket and held it. The setting light flickered on it.

Outside, a dog barked on the ridge.

I was alarmed by a woman's voice, "Webster, come!"

Soon after, the greenhouse door opened.

"Sit, Webster," a woman commanded. "Are you here to buy apples, Mister?"

By the sound of her voice, I knew who it was before I even turned around.

The dog barked.

"Quiet, Webster."

"Annie?"

"Oh, my God! Willy!" she said, noticing the black rock in my hands. It's okay, Webster. He's a friend."

"I would have called you, Annie, but I forgot your number in Amsterdam."

"I tried calling your number there, but all I got was a recorded message. This number's been disconnected."

"I moved out and had to come back to New York short notice—my father passed away last week."

"Oh, I'm really sorry to hear that, Willy."

"Thanks. He had a heart problem," I explained while Annie came up to me, and we hugged each other. "I finally found you."

"That you have. C'mon, it'll be dark soon. We'll go down to the house. You can meet my aunt and uncle."

We left the glass house as the setting sun turned the western sky a deep pink red, purple and violet. I glanced at it a moment.

Annie and I held hands as we hiked the ridge, and down into the orchard. The dog swiftly ran ahead of us. I stopped to drink some water.

"I tried finding you in Manhattan, Annie. Spent the last four days searching for you. Then I remembered you said your aunt and uncle had an apple orchard in Marlboro."

"It's good you remembered," she said as we watched the moon rise over the trees. She pulled me close, and we kissed.

"How long are you visiting your aunt and uncle?"

"I'm not visiting them—I live here now. I'm helping them run the farm. I moved out of the city three days ago."

Annie showed me inside the yellow farmhouse and into a living room, where a middle-aged man and woman sat on a couch and watched the Wheel of Fortune.

"Aunt Tess—Uncle Ed?"

"Yes, Annie?"

"I found the person who was in the orchard. He's someone I know."

"He wanna buy some apples?" the man asked. "Got plenty for sale."

"Hello."

"This is my Uncle Ed and Aunt Tess. This is Willy."

"It's nice to meet you, Willy," the man said.

Annie's aunt smiled and bashfully ducked into the kitchen.

I went over to shake the man's calloused hand, and he announced his full name: "Ed Rosenfeld. I'm mighty pleased to meet ya."

"Willy Maze. It's nice to meet you."

"Annie is your friend staying for dinner?" the woman inquired while she poked her head from the kitchen.

"I don't know, Aunty. Are you Willy?"

"I really should be going. I'll have to take a raincheck."

"Drive safe then," the older woman said.

I bid them a good evening, and Annie walked me out to the car. She gave me a slip of paper with a number on it.

"It's the phone number here. Don't lose it this time."

"I won't."

"Call me tomorrow night," she said. "I'll have time to talk."

"Annie?"

"Yeah?"

"When you first told me you danced for a living, I never would've guessed you were . . ."

"A stripper?"

"That's not what I meant. There's nothing shameful about it."

"I'm glad you feel that way, Willy. So, you're saying it's okay for a nice Jewish girl like me to be a stripper?"

"Annie . . ."

"How'd you find out?"

"When I was in a deli on the Lower East Side, I met this crazy looking guy who said he'd seen you dance before. At a place called New York New York."

"You mean that nut case at Katz's Deli?"

"Yeah, the guy who said he was Kramer from Seinfeld. We went over to the theater to try and find you, but they told me a woman named Annie Rose quit working there a couple days ago."

"That's my stage name, Willy. My real name is Annabel Rosenfeld."

"That doesn't change the way I feel about you, Annie."

"What's that mean?"

"I'm in love with you," I announced.

"Sounds like I heard that from a movie once or twice."

"Probably."

"Did you see a show at the New York New York?"

"No, I saw a show at the Ritz, and one at the Moulin Rouge," I replied.

"I worked at both places. Once upon a time. I quit burlesque."

"Why?"

"Don't like it. Never have."

"Why'd you do it in the first place?" I asked.

"It's a long story—I'm going inside—it's cold out here. Call me tomorrow."

Annie put her hand around the back of my neck, and she kissed me. I got behind the wheel, and she waved from the porch before I backed out of the driveway.

I coasted the entire length down Old Indian Road, got on Route 9W south, and then drove home to New Windsor.

I pulled into the driveway just when the lights went off in my mother's bedroom.

Chapter 34

The night after I discovered Annie, was the first sound sleep I had in five days. I felt like a completely different person in the morning. I dressed, came downstairs, inhaling the scent of French toast my mom had cooking.

"Morning."

"Morning, William."

"I have some terrific news for you, Mom."

"Don't tell me—you found Annie—right?"

"I did."

"See . . . I knew you would find her. Where was she?"

"In an apple orchard in Marlboro."

"I thought she lived in Manhattan. What was she doing there?"

"Her aunt and uncle have an orchard in Marlboro. She moved out of the city and came up to help her relatives with the farm."

"I'm happy you finally found her."

"Me too."

"When are you going to see her again?"

"I don't know—she told me to call her tonight."

Chapter 35

On a blustery Saturday afternoon, I picked up Annie at Stonybrook Farm, and we headed to my mom's house for dinner. On the way down we heard on the car radio that later in the evening, a rare celestial event would be happening: the planets Mars, Jupiter, Uranus, Neptune, Venus and Saturn would be aligned in the night sky.

"Maybe we'll be able to see it from the attic at my mother's house."

"Not without a good telescope," Annie stated.

"There's one up there. Studying the stars and the planets is one of her hobbies. That and needlepoint."

"That's pretty cool," Annie said while she glanced toward the old ballpark on Union Ave. Tall weeds had sprouted in the outfield; the tennis court had been turned into a parking lot.

"I played baseball there, once upon a time."

I crossed the train tracks, drove up the hill, turned left onto Oak Street, and then waved to some old neighbors before pulling into a driveway.

"We're here," I announced.

"Pretty house."

"It is. I'll get the apples—you bring the wine."

I took a wooden box out of the trunk while Annie grabbed her purse and a bottle. She stood by the car and looked at the brick, split-level house a few moments.

"What's the matter?"

"Maybe your mother won't like me, Willy."

"Why wouldn't she like you?"

"Because I worked as a stripper."

"She doesn't know that," I stated. "Let's go inside—this box is getting heavy."

I placed the apples outside the garage, and we walked to the front door."

"Mom, we're here!"

She appeared in the living room, wearing an apron and holding a spatula. I smelled the odor of fish and fried potatoes cooking.

"Mom—this is Annie Rosenfeld."

"Hello, Mrs. Maze. It's nice to meet you."

"Good evening, Ms. Rosenfeld. It's a pleasure to meet you. That's a cute outfit."

"Thanks. I brought some wine. Hope you like white."

"I do."

"My condolences about your husband."

"Oh, thanks."

"Willy mentioned you love making applesauce and pie, so I got you a big box of apples from my aunt and uncle's orchard. It's outside."

"That's wonderful, Annie."

"Would you like a hand in the kitchen, Mrs. Maze?"

"I'm finished cooking. You can help me set the table though. Willy, why don't you get the apples in the garage before the raccoons find them."

Annie was a little nervous at first, but after a couple glasses of wine, she and mom really hit it off. Better than I expected. Dinner was a tremendous success also. Baked halibut, home-fried potatoes, a tasty Caesar salad, and warmed apple pie with vanilla ice cream. Annie and mom got to know each other while I cleared and loaded the dishwasher.

"You have a beautiful last name, Annie," my mother said.

"Thanks. Rosenfeld means field of roses."

"Where's your family from?"

"My parents were born in the Ukraine. Kiev," Annie replied. "They came here after World War Two. By ship to Ellis Island. My dad's name was Abraham. My mom's name was Esther. Like Queen Esther from the bible. God, she was such an amazing woman! Pretty. Excuse me, I get a little choked up when I talk about them. They died in a plane crash when I was thirteen."

"I'm sorry. Get her a tissue, Willy. How'd you become a dancer?"

"I started taking ballet classes in Florida when I was five. I loved it. By the time I turned 11, my dance instructor encouraged me to pursue a career in ballet. I followed her advice."

"Do you like cognac, Annie?" my mother asked.

"Yeah."

"Willy, get the bottle and three glasses out of the cabinet, please. Perhaps you should stay the night, Annie. Willy shouldn't be driving under the influence. He's already had a beer and two glasses of wine."

"I agree, Mrs. Maze."

"I have a spare guest room you can sleep in," my mother spoke.

"Can I use your phone?—I'll call my Aunt Tess—so she won't be worried about me."

"There's one in the kitchen, dear."

While Annie used the phone, I set three glasses on the dining room table and poured the cognac. My mother whispered to me: "Your girlfriend is precious, Willy. She's a beautiful woman."

"Now you know why I was so determined to find her."

Annie hung up the phone, and she returned to the dining room. "She said it was okay."

"Great. I'd like to propose a toast," I said while lifting my glass. "To a happy and healthy life for all of us."

"To a happy and healthy life for all of us," Annie and my mother repeated. We knocked our glasses together and drank.

"I'd love to hear more about your story, Ms. Rosenfeld."

"Oh—it's really not that interesting—Mrs. Maze."

"I'm sure it is. Come on."

Annie drank some cognac, looked across the table at me with her big blue eyes and smiled. I smiled back, and gave her an assuring look.

"All right then. When I was twelve years old and attending middle school in Florida, some people came and watched me dance ballet in a school recital. We were putting on the Nutcracker. Afterward, a woman gave me her business card, and told me to contact her when I got to high school. After my mom and dad passed away, I moved in with my aunt and uncle at the farm in Marlboro. I continued dance lessons throughout middle and high school. During my second year of high school, I called the number the woman had given me, and the Julliard School asked if I would be interested in giving them a private recital at my school. I did. They were extremely impressed, and awarded me a four-year scholarship for dance. I accepted their offer."

"That must've been fun going there," I said.

"It was extremely challenging, but I loved every minute of it. That's my class ring from Julliard, Mrs. Maze."

My mother held Annie's hand, and she admired her ring. "Now that's an accomplishment you must be proud of."

"It definitely is."

"Willy worked as a professional clarinetist on Broadway and in Amsterdam."

"I know. He told me all about it," Annie said.

"What did you do after you graduated Julliard?" my mother asked.

"I was offered a job dancing with the New York City Ballet Company. I was with them for three years. And worked with some of the best dancers and choreographers in the world. In 1979, I danced in my first Broadway musical. *A Chorus Line*. In 1980, our production company did a world tour for a year. After the tour, my contract ended. And I started working on 42nd Street. I'm only kidding. I tell that to everybody. I mean the musical, *42nd Street*. I was a lead dancer in the show for a full season. And that was the last Broadway musical I danced in."

"Why?" Mom inquired.

"I was on a vacation in Colorado, and had a really bad skiing accident."

"What happened?"

"I tore my left meniscus and broke my right ankle in two places."

"How unfortunate."

"Extremely. After I had knee surgery and my ankle healed, about eight months later, I tried going back to dancing, but it just didn't work anymore. That's when I got into performing shows in burlesque theaters. I only did it to pay my bills. I never cared for exposing myself like that."

I'm surprised she let the cat out of the bag. I thought to myself.

"It's nothing to be ashamed of," my mother said. I would've probably done the same thing if I were in your shoes. Well, that's certainly a fabulous story, Annie. But I'll be turning into a pumpkin soon, if I don't go to bed. Why don't you show her where she's gonna sleep, Willy. The beds already made. And there's some clean pajamas and a bath towel and wash cloth for her on the dresser."

"You hear about the planets, Mom?"

"I did."

"Can we take a look through your telescope?"

"Sure. Don't know if you'll see anything tonight. It's a little overcast. And be careful with it."

"I will."

"Good night, Mrs. Maze. And thanks again for that lovely dinner."

"You're welcome."

After showing Annie the guest room, we brought our cognacs up to the finished attic, sat on chairs there, and then aimed my mother's telescope through a window facing the eastern sky. *She was right.* There wasn't much to see, aside for some clouds and a stray star. That didn't bother us any, because we were too busy getting our own planets aligned.

Chapter 36

Two days after our get together at mom's, I was awakened by the phone in the bedroom.

"—Willy, it's Annie."

"Morning. What is it?"

"—think I left my Julliard ring at your mother's house the other night. Can't find it anywhere. Maybe I placed it on the dining room table while we were talking."

"I just opened my eyes. I'll look in a little bit."

"Please do."

After eating two soft-boiled eggs and toast, I drove to the Beacon train station and rode the 10 am express into Manhattan. I took the subway to Fifth Avenue, walked a short distance, and then found a swanky looking jewelry store called Ted & Michael's. It had a great big storefront window that displayed a variety of sparkling jewelry. I entered and browsed a case containing some expensive watches. In tight jeans, white blouse, and maroon sports jacket, an attractive looking saleswoman came up to me and graciously asked: "Welcome to Ted & Michael's, sir. Need a good watch today?"

"No, thanks. I'm seeing about an engagement ring."

"—picking it up?"

"I haven't ordered it yet."

"Would you like a coffee or a water?"

"No."

"Have a seat over there—someone in the ring department will be with you shortly. Love your hat."

"Thanks."

I sat on a plush chair and took out the little box I had in my pants pocket. I set it on the glass counter and waited a few minutes until a jeweler appeared.

A man sat opposite me and simpered a moment while glancing at my cowboy hat; I took it off and placed it on my lap.

"You tie your horse out back, partner?" the jeweler inquired in a dorky John Wayne impersonation.

"No, she's on the side next to the saloon. Morning. I'm inquiring about having an engagement ring made. I already have the diamond for it."

"I understand, sir. My name's Michael Walsh. I'm one of the owners here. And your name is?"

"Willy Maze."

Mr. Walsh asked while pointing to the little box with his fat index finger; an ugly pink wart grew on his middle knuckle. "Is the diamond in there?"

"It is."

"Well, let's have a look at it, cowboy," the jeweler said in another snarky impersonation.

"Excuse me?"

"The diamond, Mr. Maze."

"I'm not a cowboy, Mr. Walsh."

"I was only joking. I apologize. Didn't mean to offend you."

"Accepted."

When I opened the hinged box, a saffron-yellow light came through the storefront window, as if the sun's rays had shined in, but it couldn't be possible, because the sun was facing the stores on the other side of 5th Avenue. Astonished pedestrians paused in front of the jewelry store window — their mouths agape — staring inside.

"Wow, that's some diamond!" the jeweler declared while another jeweler, a customer nearby, the saleswoman in the maroon sports jacket, and a security guard all turned their heads toward the loud announcement.

"It should make a nice ring for my fiancé. What do you think, Mr. Walsh?"

"Absolutely, sir. Let's take a closer look at it."

The jeweler carefully lifted the precious gem and examined it through his magnifier a few moments. His jaw dropped and looking eye widened. He excitedly called to another jeweler: "You gotta see this rock, Jim!"

"What's the matter?" I asked.

"It happens to be an extremely rare diamond, Mr. Maze. There aren't many in the world like it."

"Oh, yeah?"

"Mr. Maze, this is my colleague and co-owner, Jim Brady. He'll give us a second opinion."

"It's nice to meet you," the co-owner said.

"Likewise."

Mr. Brady sat down and observed the gem through his handheld scope.

"What do you think, Jim?" his colleague inquired.

"It's extraordinary. Where'd you get this diamond, Mr. Maze?"

"It was a gift. How much would it cost to have an engagement ring made from it? A ballpark figure."

"My colleague and I will have to consult about it in private a few moments. Pardon the inconvenience."

"No problem. I'll hold the diamond," I said, taking it and placing it back inside the small box.

A couple minutes later, the store owners returned and sat down.

Mr. Brady broadly smiled while his business partner cleared his throat: "Mr. Maze, I don't know where you acquired such an exceptional diamond, but from what we've gathered, it happens to be worth a good sum of money. It wouldn't be practical for us to make a simple engagement ring from it."

"Why not?"

"Because we're prepared to offer you a price," Mr. Brady replied.

"For what?"

"The diamond, of course," Mr. Walsh added. "Our jewelry store wants to purchase it from you."

"I didn't come here to sell it."

"We'll give you $50,000 for the diamond," Mr. Walsh said. "I can have an official bank check ready for you in 45 minutes."

I looked at the two men, closed the box, and then put it into my pants pocket. I brushed a piece of lint off my rancher's hat, and placed it on my head.

"What do you say, Mr. Maze?"

"I told you, I'm not interested in selling the diamond."

I stood, and prepared to leave the store.

"We'll give you $75,000 for it," Mr. Brady earnestly spoke.

"I appreciate your time. Have a good day, gentlemen."

"One hundred thousand dollars cash, Mr. Maze!" Mr. Walsh spurted. "It'll be in your hands in less than one hour."

I made eye contact with the man, tipped my hat, and then winked. "No thanks, cowboy. Excuse me, I have to give my horse some water."

After having a hamburger and fries near Grand Central, I took the train back to Beacon and drove to Newburgh.

I discovered a small jewelry shop on Liberty Street, across from George Washington's Headquarters. It was called Cohen's. And owned by an old Jewish man named Irv.

I entered the cluttered store, showed the owner my diamond, and he unemotionally viewed it with his antique magnifier.

"Very nice," he said. "Lovely in fact."

"I want an engagement ring made from it. Can you give me a price?"

"Okay. And then okay," he said amusingly. "You vanna hear a joke first, mister?"

"Sure, why not."

Mr. Cohen drank some cold coffee. And looked at me.

'Two old men, Abe and Louie. Are sitting in Central Park. Abe asks: 'do you think there's baseball in heaven, Louie?'

'I don't know, Abe. That's a good question. I'll tell you what. Whoever dies first, should come back in a dream and tell whoever is still living if they play baseball in heaven, or not,' Louie said.

'Fair enough.'

'Unfortunately, Louie had a stroke a month later and kicked the bucket. One night while Abe slept, Louie visited him in a dream: 'Abe . . . it's Louie.'

'Where are you? What is it?' Abe tiredly asked.

'I'm in heaven. And I have some good news and some bad news for you.'

'Yes?'

'The good news is—they have baseball in heaven.'

'That's wonderful!' Abe exclaimed. 'So what could be the bad news?' he questioned Louie from the dream.

'The bad news is—you're pitching Friday, Abe.'

"That's pretty funny, Mr. Cohen. I have to remember that one. So what about the ring?"

"I can easily arrange that for you, Mr. Maze. Do you have the size of the ring finger?"

"It's right here," I replied handing him Annie's graduation ring from Julliard, I had clandestinely borrowed the night she slept at my mom's house.

The jeweler measured the exact circumference of the ring, showed me what he had for bands, and the designs to choose from.

I decided upon a style, and with no hassles or melodrama, Mr. Cohen told me what the price would be: $1,000. I left the diamond with him, and in four days' time, I returned to the store and paid him for a spectacular looking wedding ring. I told him if it all worked out, I'd buy two gold bands from him in the near future.

On Annie's day off from doing the books for the orchard, she and I went to the Ship Lantern Inn for lunch.

"It's a gorgeous afternoon," she said while we looked inside the menus.

"For sure."

I watched while Annie rubbed her bare ring finger.

"Did you see if my Julliard ring was at your mom's house, Willy? It means a lot to me. I'd hate to lose it."

"Of course not. I believe my mother put it by the phone," I said while the maître de came to the table with a bouquet of red roses.

"These just arrived for you, Mr. Maze."

"Thank you."

"Who are those for?" Annie inquired.

"You. Can we get two glasses of champagne, please," I told the waitress while handing Annie the red bouquet.

"What are we celebrating?"

I placed a little hinged-box on the table and opened it. Annie looked at the diamond ring inside. She was flabbergasted.

"Oh, my God!"

The dining room brightened with the same yellowish-gold light I saw in Amsterdam and the jewelry store in Manhattan.

I held Annie's hand.

"Will you marry me?"

She gazed far into my eyes a moment.

"Only if you give me back my Julliard ring."

"Here," I said.

"I had a funny feeling you had it, Willy."

I slipped the engagement ring onto Annie's finger. And just then, the light in the room shined even brighter. She raised her hand and admired the diamond.

"Of course I'll marry you, Willy."

"Lord! That's the most amazing ring I've ever seen," the waitress exclaimed as she set the Champagne down, and just about knocked over one of the glasses.

Chapter 37

While Annie and I rocked on the front porch at Stonybrook Farm, we watched the last mottled red, yellow and orange leaves fall from the old oak tree by the barn, and the branches were left completely barren. We were in love. And we had the rest of our lives ahead of us.

"When do you wanna get married, William?"

"June might be a good month."

"It's the end of October. We've got plenty of time to plan for the wedding."

"June will be here in no time, Annie."

A dervish-like breeze stirred up the dead leaves on the ground, as the oak branches freely swayed. We heard the voice of the Indian spirit just then.

"There's that sound again, Willy."

"I've heard it before. At the park in Newburgh."

"It's a bit scary," Annie said. "Like it's warning us about something."

"You think? It probably doesn't get too exciting around here on Halloween," I mentioned.

"Not really. The only places where children might go trick or treating are here, the Buford's, and Ezekial Smith's house across the road. They keep to themselves. I hear his wife scream a lot. And Monday, she was burning something awful smelling in the backyard."

"I took Webster for a walk past their house the other day, and Mr. Smith looked at me like he wanted to kill me," I said.

"I wouldn't go too near their property, Willy. They're nothing but trouble. Last time I actually saw either of them close up was on Halloween, seventeen years ago."

"Really?"

"I was thirteen. My aunt and uncle took me trick-or-treating into Marlboro. I was dressed as Snow White and having a really fun time until we returned home, and I went over to the Smith's house for candy. My aunt and uncle waited in the car while I rang their doorbell. Mrs. Smith opened the door, and she was wearing a long black dress. I said happy Halloween, and gazed up at her angry face while waiting for her to put some candy into my bag."

"So?"

"Blood was dripping from her hands and arms."

"Was it fake blood?"

"I didn't stay long enough to ask. She tried to pull me inside the house, but she ripped my costume halfway off in the process. I was so scared, I dropped my bag of candy and ran back to the car as fast as I could."

"Where was Mr. Smith all that time?"

"Standing in the front yard. Yelling trick-or-treat, bitch! Trick or treat! That's not all he was doing."

"What do you mean?"

"He pulled down his pants and shined a moon. Then he pissed on the front lawn. We all saw him do it from the car before Uncle Ed backed out of their driveway."

"What a sick bastard."

"Yeah. Creepy. Blood was all over my white costume. Boy—were my aunt and uncle mad at them."

"What did they do about it?"

"Nothing. None of us ever spoke to them again. It's time to eat—let's go inside."

That night, the temperature dropped to the low thirties on the hill above Old Indian Road; a heavy frost collected in the orchard.

Down in the valley, a macabre Halloween moon ascended above the shadowy Hudson.

It turned midnight. Annie and I covered ourselves with an extra blanket.

Mr. Rosenfeld added more wood to the fireplace in the living room before sitting down and lighting his pipe.

His wife retired to her bedroom.

At a house in Marlboro, a teen-age boy stole a bottle of whiskey and the keys to his father's car. He picked up two friends, and they drank a six-pack and the pint of whiskey on a drive up Old Indian Road. They drunkenly stopped at an orchard to piss and have a brief apple fight before the boy behind the wheel pulled into Ezekial Smith's driveway and swallowed the last drops of whiskey; they got out, and the driver smashed the glass bottle in the bed of Mr. Smith's pickup.

The porch light went on, and the rowdy teens pelted the front door with raw eggs and rotten apples. They approached the house, and pressed the doorbell several times while taunting 'trick or treat'.

They heard someone question nearby: "Do you want some candy little boys?"

Dressed in a long black dress, Jezebel Smith, walked up behind the youths, and she smashed a burning jack-o'-lantern onto the head of one of the teens while Ezekial Smith opened the door, wearing a Clint Eastwood mask and holding a sawed-off shot gun. He pointed it at the three youths, and they thought it was a joke and laughed.

The man loaded the gun.

"Make my day!" he shouted.

The teen age boys ran to the car, but it was too late. Mr. Smith pulled the trigger, and hit one of them in the back; another kid was shot in the leg while they got inside the vehicle. Mr. and Mrs. Smith laughed while they closed the front door and went inside the house.

The boy driving the car was doing 75 mph down Old Indian Road when they reached the intersection of Route 9 South; the driver of a tractor trailer broadsided the father's car, and it was thrown into the woods and burst into flames.

The next morning in the kitchen, Ed Rosenfeld turned on the radio while his wife poured coffee into his favorite cup.

"I heard gunshots last night, Tess. Sounded like it came from across the road."

"I was fast asleep," his wife stated.

"What time was that, Ed?" I asked while entering the kitchen in my pajamas. Annie stood beside me.

"About thirty minutes past midnight, Willy. Right after I walked the dog."

"I heard it too," Annie mentioned. "Thought it was fireworks."

"Oh, it wasn't fireworks, Annie," her uncle stated.

The man on the radio said there was little left of the car the three boys were in. They were burned beyond recognition while the truck driver had been taken to the hospital with head injuries and was paralyzed from the waist down.

Chapter 38

Winter finally ended at Stonybrook Farm, and the overflowing stream gushed down the hill, and into the thawing Hudson.

On April Fool's Day, Webster was vomiting and lethargic so much, Annie and I drove him to the vet. The doctor said he might have ingested some rat poison. I told him it couldn't have come from the farm, because Mr. Rosenfeld was strictly against using any kind of chemicals or poisonous substances in the orchard. We figured it had to be from Ezekial Smith's property; Webster had the habit of running over there recently. We brought him home, and the dog died two days after. He was buried in the clearing up the hill from the orchard, not far from the old round greenhouse nearby the flowering blueberry bushes.

Uncle Ed and Aunt Tess adopted two puppies. A male and female German Short-haired Pointers. Two out of eight puppies plus the mother that were abandoned by the cruel neighbors across the road. Ed and I brought the other six pups and the mother to the animal shelter, where they eventually found homes.

On one balmy Spring morning while taking a couple boxes of apples to the woman who owned the country store on 9W, I encountered an adult, short haired pointer who appeared dead in a ditch at the bottom of Old Indian Road. I got out of my truck and read a message attached to the male dog's collar. *You forgot about this one asshole.*

Chapter 39

On June 26, 1984, Annie and I got married at The Hotel Newburgh on lower Broadway. Johnstone flew in from California to be my best man while Mrs. Ben Gurion came all the way from Kfar Shalem, to be the ring bearer. My mother, and my father's brother, Uncle Seymore Maze, accompanied me dressed in a shiny black tux, tie, and white rose pinned to our lapels. I waited under the wedding canopy while a pianist played in the background. It was a sunny Summer day.

Annie had a couple of her long-time friends she used to dance with, as her bridesmaids; a proud Uncle Ed and Aunt Tess walked her down the aisle, glowing in a white silk wedding gown, hyacinth violet veil, and gold conjugal heels. She and I stood together under the chuppah, the white wedding canopy that symbolized the home we would build together. Mrs. Ben Gurion stood nearby holding the box the wedding rings were in.

The rabbi spoke, and the ceremony commenced.

When the ring box was opened, an astounding violet light illuminated the hall. We said our vows, I kissed my bride, and then broke the shot glass under my shoe.

Shouts of 'mazel tov' filled the room.

After we honeymooned a week in Hawaii, Annie and I flew back to New York. I packed the rest of my belongings at my mother's place, and permanently moved into the big yellow farmhouse in Marlboro.

Three months later, my wife got pregnant.

In May of 1985, she gave birth to twins. A son and daughter. Hillel and Estelle Maze. Hilly and Esty as they preferred to be called.

The children grew up fast. And pretty soon, they were helping out with the chores around the farm, feeding the chickens, gathering eggs, picking blueberries, apples, and working in the vegetable garden.

Uncle Ed taught our little boy how to ferment cabbage and cucumbers, and they made some of the best darn kosher pickles and sauerkraut in the state.

Aunt Tess taught our young daughter how to make apple butter and tomato sauce, canning it in bell jars and shelving it in the cool cellar. Esty was always in the kitchen with Aunt Tess, or in my mom's kitchen, learning how to bake and cook from the time she was three.

When the farm lay dormant in the winter months, we took trips down to my mom's house, and my wife and I brought the kids to Downing Park, where we ice skated on the pond. When there was a good cover of snow on the ground, we would take them sleigh riding down the big hill at Epiphany College in New Windsor. Dozens of people were there.

On Spring afternoons, after school and homework, Hilly would help Uncle Ed and I work in the orchard. At 10-years-old, the boy knew how to drive the tractor, plant trees, prune, and pick apples. Because all of us worked very hard at the farm, everyone was blessed with a veritable Garden of Eden.

Our son and daughter eventually grew up, attended elementary, high school, college, and then started their own families.

Annie and I became grandparents, and my mother became a great grandmother. She lived to a ripe old age of 99. Uncle Ed was 97 when he passed, and Aunt Tess died two years later at 102.

My wife and I lived the good life on Stonybrook Farm, and we eventually grew old together. Into the twenty-first century.

Chapter 40

In the early morning before daybreak, Wildman, our German Short-haired Pointer, crazily howled in the back yard while Annie and I slept. I got out of bed, dressed, and then went outside to see what the commotion was about.

"What's the matter Wildman?—you see some racoons?"

The large brown dog looked at me puzzled; he pointed his wet snout at the clear black sky in the west and barked again: I was startled when I saw an enormous full moon, glowing a radiant blue, almost the shade of Annie's eyes.

"So, that's what you're barking at. C'mon, boy. It's only the moon. Let's go for a walk."

I knew then, that 29th of June in 2026, would be like no other day in my life.

The dog sniffed as many wildflowers as he could while we hiked to the ridge above the farm.

I paused to observe the river, then watched a speck of scarlet brightness appear over Mt. Beacon.

When the dog and I returned home, the sun had climbed higher in the sky, leaving a faint blue impression of the lunar body.

I poured water into the dog's bowl and wiped off my wet shoes before going inside the house.

"Morning, Annie."

"Morning. You're up early. I'm making blueberry pancakes. Last of the frozen berries Esty's and Hilly's kids picked last summer."

"Great, I'm hungry. There was a really strange moon out this morning."

"Oh yeah? Why don't you take a shower, William. Breakfast will be ready by the time you're done."

After we ate, Annie and I brought our coffees to the front porch, where we enjoyed the view of the late blossoming apple trees while rocking on the chairs we purchased from a Cracker Barrel in Gulf Shores Alabama. We loved sitting on those chairs, rocking underneath the firmament day or night. (Like we could do that forever.) There were times in bygone summers, I would transport the chairs up the hill overlooking the Hudson: my wife and I would rock all night, watch the sky, the boats on the water, and tell stories to each other till the rooster crowed.

We finished our coffees, and Annie did some work in the herb garden while I washed the breakfast dishes, made the bed, and then swept the house.

I dusted off my old clarinet case, put the instrument together, and then played it underneath the oak tree by the barn. While blowing a tune, the oak leaves rustled, and I heard the chanting of the old Indian spirit again. I listened awhile as a cloud drifted in front of the sun.

A strong gust of wind came up from the north, and it shook the oak trees in ours and Ezekial Smith's yard. The wind increased while the local woodpeckers ended their hammering. Sparrows, robins, finches, bluebirds and crows hastily flew off. Our dog, cat, squirrels, hedgehogs and a lone box turtle raised their heads in question— before bolting to God knows where.

Annie removed her gardening gloves and raised her hand to admire her diamond wedding ring. She never wore it while working in the garden, but she did that day. From above, a kaleidoscopic brilliance reflected off the gem, and she stood there utterly amazed.

Blacker than a blacksmith's anvil, a cloud blocked the sun. A luminescent azure sky was everywhere else, yet I heard the distinct sound of thunder. The Indian spirit chanted louder; the rain poured onto the garden and Annie undoubtedly got soaked. I heard her laughing.

The rain passed, and a broad rainbow arched across the heavens. I saw it from the porch.

My wife shouted: "Do you see the rainbow, William?"

"I see it, Annie. Never seen one quite like that before."

Meanwhile, an incandescent flame shot rapidly in the sky, and a fire landed on the ground in front of me; it briefly scorched the grass, and then a mysterious looking man appeared. He wore a shimmering white robe, a lengthy head of hair and beard hung from his youthful face; a colorful skull cap like my own, covered his head. I wasn't scared. I met him a long time ago, but couldn't recall where. In one hand he held a smooth black stone. In the other, a sheet of paper with many words written on it.

"Can I help you with something?" I inquired.

"Are you Willy Maze?"

"Yes, I am."

"I've come to deliver a most important message."

"What's that?"

"I am the prophet of great wisdom, truth, love and compassion. If you remember . . . when you were a young man, I told you I would visit again when you were older. It's that time."

"Now I recall! I met you when I was at the music festival in Woodstock. 1969. My guardian spirit was with me then."

"Exactly. I will tell you what will happen on the earth," the bearded prophet spoke. "On this day, a great transformation will take place throughout the world. The seeds have been planted. The good and the bad seed. Those who have sown the good seed and have obeyed the Lord's commandments like you and your family, will be written in the book of life. Those who have planted the bad seed and performed evil actions, will harvest a whirlwind of sorrow."

My wife yelled from the garden, "William!"

"Yes, Annie?"

"We have visitors."

"Great God in heaven!" I declared while seeing an angelic-like being land in the yard. It possessed a large-winged insect torso, a human shaped head and face, orbicular eyes that threw high beams of light, like the headlights of an automobile; and its massive hands, arms, legs and feet were five times the size of an average adult man or woman.

"Holy heaven! If you're an angel you sure don't look very happy," I stated.

"I am not happy," the strange being said as its amplified voice blew our wet laundry off the clothesline and broke several branches on the surrounding trees.

The visitor spread its wings, flew into the air, and then joined the other visitors that had swarmed throughout the orchard and the ridge above the Hudson.

"Do not fear, Mr. Maze," the white-robed prophet said. "That is one of God's good messengers."

The locust-like beings passed over our farmhouse, and the prophet and I watched two of the harbingers stop in front of Ezekial Smith's front door; they knocked and rang the bell. His pickup truck was in the driveway, yet no one answered. One of the messengers stepped back, opened its mouth, and then let out a shout that echoed across the valley: "Mr. Smith! Are you home?"

Still, no one came to the door.

Both messengers opened their mouths, and they blew the door off the hinges, tore the windows, walls, and roof from the house while old and angry Ezekial Smith and his wicked wife, Jezebel, ignored the loud windstorm. They sat naked in the living room, watching a wide-screen TV at full volume; every inch of their wrinkled bodies covered in diabolical symbols.

The two messengers approached the sinful husband and wife, and they looked up in surprise at the uninvited callers. Mrs. Smith showed them her middle finger. And the prophet and I watched as the winged messengers picked them up and flew into the sky. Our next-door neighbors were never seen, or heard from again.

My wife ran to the front porch. "Willy!—a tornado just destroyed the neighbor's house."

She suddenly noticed the prophet while his bare feet threw quick sparks of lightning.

"Who is this, William?"

"Our guest, Annie. He's the prophet of love, wisdom, truth and compassion."

"Where did he come from?"

"Beyond the most distant sky," I replied.

"Don't be afraid, Mrs. Maze. I am here to tell your husband something. If you would like to stay and listen—you're quite welcome."

"Do you want something to eat or drink, kind prophet?"

"Only water, thank you."

Annie went inside the house, and shortly after, she returned with a glass and a pitcher of cold spring water from the brook. She poured the liquid into the prophet's glass, and he drank some before speaking.

"Thank you, kind woman."

"You're welcome."

The prophet looked at the paper with the words written on it.

"Billions of the Lord's messengers have arrived, Mr. and Mrs. Maze. They are everywhere on the earth by now."

"Why are they here?" I asked.

"To initiate the great transformation."

"What does that mean?" Annie inquired.

"It means that the good Lord will no longer tolerate what evil souls are doing, and have done on this planet for eons now. Time has come for the ones who insist on only doing evil, to be removed from this earth forever. The messengers are here for that purpose, and so much more. The evil ones will be required to reside on another planet altogether, and you may have heard of such a place from your holy bible. *It is called Hell*. The good Lord's messengers will find the ones who hide in dark

232

webs, and do bad things to men, women and children. Like Mr. and Mrs. Smith's fate, the messengers will do the same for millions and millions more. From this day on, communist and fascist regimes will no longer oppress and enslave people. There will be no more corrupt and oppressive governments. I will drink more water now."

While the prophet quenched his thirst, Annie and I observed a multitude of winged messengers in the sky; there were so many of them, they blocked the sun's light, and the day became night. We illuminated candles, a lantern, and the porch light.

The prophet set down his glass, and he continued to read his message:

"From this day forward, there will be no more wars fought on Mother Earth. All nations shall dismantle their military machines, nuclear bombs, missiles, jet fighters and guns. Never to be used on the planet again. Like the words go: 'your swords will be beaten into ploughshares, and man will study war no more'. All technology harmful to humans and creatures will stop. Industries that make toxic materials will be closed forever. Laboratories and pharmaceutical companies who produce and distribute deadly drugs and other substances will close as well. The good Lord's children will not perish from these substances any longer. Corporations who profit by harming man, animals, birds, insects, ocean life, or the environment, shall permanently be out of business. This includes companies that manufacture cigarettes, alcoholic beverages, processed foods, white sugar, plastic, etc. Man's exploration of outer space is finished. The earth's cluttered orbit will be cleaned of its satellites and other junk. Special teachers will come to the planet, and instruct men, women and children on how to clean and rid the earth of all its air and water pollution, plastic, toxic fuels, chemicals, oils, and so forth. People will learn how to use herbs and plants to heal themselves and prevent disease. Food will be your medicine. There will be many more changes on the planet."

The prophet paused to rest while Annie refilled his glass. He drank again.

"Billions of school children and adults will plant trees in the rainforests and other forests of the world. This way, the good earth can supply man and beast with a fresh and plentiful supply of oxygen once more. The oceans, lakes, rivers, and streams shall be made pure again. Everyone in the world will learn how to grow gardens for food, so they can all thrive and be healthy human beings. There will be no more starvation on the planet. Mankind's slaughterhouses will close also. The cruel practice of killing and eating the Lord's animals has ended. They have suffered long enough. Your schools and colleges will stop teaching harmful theories, hatred, racial and religious prejudices. There won't ever be a need for prisons, jails, courts, judges, or lawyers."

"Why is that?" I inquired.

"Because crime and criminals will never have a place on this earth again. Children and adults will learn about healing, love, mindfulness, and the respect for all human life and nature. There will be no more dangerous medical operations to alter the sex of adults or children. This practice has been an abomination to the Creator of the infinite universes. Nobody on the planet will own more than anyone else. All will be given an equal share of abundance. And that abundance shall be shared by all. Money will no longer be used to pay for things. People will barter again. And give and receive from the goodness of their hearts. No one will endure hardship, enslavement and persecution ever again. All people will have a place to call home. A planet shared and cherished by all. There will be no more rulers, no more politicians and governments, no more countries, and no more borders. Only a planet, where people cooperate and work with each other, practicing true love and a vision for eternal peace. That is all I have to say, Mr. and Mrs. Maze. It is time for me to leave, and for the great transformation to unfold."

The prophet stood, put his hands over our heads, and then gave us his blessing. Afterward, we watched as he ascended into the sky and turn into a bright orange light, till there was nothing.

On a breezy autumn morning after the world had been changed, with our dog by our side, my wife and I faced the east, raised our arms in the air, and then gave thanks and praises to the Lord All Mighty.

The next day, Annie and I, our son and daughter, in-laws, and grandchildren harvested bushels of vegetables, herbs, and melons from the garden. We baked a thousand loaves of bread, many apple, blueberry and blackberry pies, cooked large pots of grains and beans, and then prepared a feast like no other. We invited family, friends, neighbors, strangers, and guests from near and far.

Everyone sat at long tables on the lawns throughout Stonybrook Farm. The food was brought out. We held hands, closed our eyes, and then said a prayer for the meal. We ate.

Afterward, we sang, played musical instruments and danced until day light.

And all the people on the earth were blessed with a good life. Forever and ever.

Other paperback, audio, and E-books by the author

If Frogs Could Fly
written under the pseudonym E.B. Mendel

The Help of Angels
'A historical novel with an unearthly twist'

sunbridgebooks@gmail.com

Acknowledgements

Book cover art, Geometric Landscapes, was created in 1567 by Lorenz Stoer. Courtesy of the public domain.

Book cover design by Tim Barber dissectdesigns.com

Interior formatting of E-book and print manuscript courtesy of Jennette Green from Diamond Press

The poem, Sitting with Shame written by Elisa Cobb

The lyrics in Chapter 34 were written by Kate Wolf, from her song *These Times We're Living In*. courtesy of Max Wolf.

"An energetic and enjoyable read"
Cathi Hill
The first woman mayor of Islamorada, Florida

"A most intriguing story"
Mary Havard
A retired teacher and nurse